WARPED GALAXIES

SECRETS OF THE

TAU

STORIES FROM THE FAR FUTURE

WARPED GALAXIES

Book 1 ATTACK OF THE NECRON (Out Now)

Book 2 CLAWS OF THE GENESTEALER (Out Now)

Book 3 SECRETS OF THE TAU (Out Now)

Book 4 WAR OF THE ORKS (November 2019)

STORIES IN AN AGE OF FANTASY

REALM QUEST

Book 1 CITY OF LIFESTONE (Out Now)

Book 2 LAIR OF THE SKAVEN (Out Now)

Book 3 FOREST OF THE ANCIENTS (Out Now)

Book 4 FLIGHT OF THE KHARADRON (November 2019)

SECRETS OF THE

CAVAN SCOTT

WARHAMMER ADVENTURES

First published in Great Britain in 2019 by
Warhammer Publishing,
Willow Road,
Nottingham, NG7 2WS, UK.

10 9 8 7 6 5 4 3 2 1

Produced by Games Workshop in Nottingham.
Cover illustration by Cole Marchetti.
Internal illustrations by Magnus Norén & Cole Marchetti.

A CIP record for this book is available from the British Library.

ISBN 13: 978 1 78496 839 7

See Warhammer Adventures on the internet at

warhammeradventures.com

Find out more about Games Workshop and the worlds of
Warhammer 40,000 and Warhammer Age of Sigmar at

games-workshop.com

Printed and bound by CPI Group (UK) Ltd, Croydon, CR0 4YY

For Clare.

Contents

The Imperium
of the Far Future

Life in the 41st millennium is hard.
Ruled by the Emperor of Mankind
from his Golden Throne on Terra,
humans have spread across the
galaxy, inhabiting millions of planets.
They have achieved so much, from
space travel to robotics, and yet
billions live in fear. The universe
seems a dangerous place, teeming
with alien horrors and dark powers.
But it is also a place bristling with
adventure and wonder, where battles
are won and heroes are forged.

CHAPTER ONE

Escape

The monsters were coming. They were scrambling up the towering mushroom-trees, their claws slicing into the mottled trunks. Zelia didn't know which way to run. She had scuttling aliens to the back of her and a heavily armed spaceship to the front. A woman stood on the gangplank, her longcoat billowing in the wind. She wore a curved sword in a scabbard, a beamer slung low on her waist. Her fingers were covered with rings, and her long brown hair was swept back beneath a tri-cornered hat.

'Who are you?' Zelia asked as the

woman stared at them incredulously.

'Who cares?' Talen snapped at her, before turning to the newcomer.
'We're about to be lunch. There are Genestealers on their way... Lots of Genestealers.'

'So it would appear,' the woman said as one of the creatures scrambled into view. It hissed, its long tongue tasting the air. 'Get on the ship.'

Talen was right – introductions could wait.

'Don't look at its eyes,' the woman shouted, running back up the gangplank. She snatched up her beamer and fired, the bolt hitting the Genestealer in the chest. It was thrown over the edge, its howl echoing through the forest.

The danger wasn't over. The rest of the pack were closing in fast.

'Move,' the woman commanded, stepping aside so the children could race up the boarding ramp.

'You don't have to tell us twice,'

Talen said, pelting up the gangplank, Zelia and Mekki following close behind. Fleapit brought up the rear, running on all fours.

All the time, the woman was firing, picking off Genestealers as they scrabbled over the edge. She only paused as Fleapit scampered past.

'Is that a...?' she began, before deciding that conversation was best left for now. 'Never mind.'

She turned to bolt up the ramp, the monsters at her heels.

Talen looked around, spotting a barrel near the wall. It clanged as he yanked it over on its side and kicked it down the gangplank. It rolled down the ramp, taking the Genestealers with it.

'Clever boy,' the woman said, slapping a control at the top of the slope. The ramp swung up, shutting the monsters out. 'Although next time try not to waste a barrel of promethium, eh?'

'You'd rather I let them in?' Talen snapped back.

'Oh, I like you.' She turned and sprinted through the ship. 'But that won't keep them out for long. Come on.'

The children followed her, chasing through arched corridors to emerge onto a pristine flight deck.

Zelia was impressed. Her mother's ship, the *Scriptor*, was a ramshackle affair, held together by rust and clutter. In contrast, the woman's flight deck was spotless, gleaming cogitator terminals edged with shining brass. The deck plates were polished and the lume-globes bright. Even the seats were covered in the finest grox-leather.

It was perfect, except for one small detail.

'Where are your crew?' Zelia asked. A ship this size should have been full of people, each station on the flight deck manned. Instead, the only other soul – if you could call it that – was a mindless servitor standing dumbly in the corner. The woman didn't even acknowledge its presence, which wasn't surprising. According to official records, servitors were vat-grown clones, their limbs replaced by cybernetic parts. Barely more than walking lumps of muscle, they were used for manual labour all across the Imperium and always gave Zelia the creeps. There was something about their eyes... so dull and lifeless. And of course there were the rumours of what... or rather *who*... they *really* were.

Striding across the deck, the woman threw her hat through the air. It landed on the servitor's chrome-plated head. The cyborg didn't even flinch.

She dropped behind the flight controls and primed the engines. The deck plates trembled as the plasma drives kicked in, although the only sound was the rasp of claws trying to slice through the ceramite hull.

'Hold on to something,' the woman barked as she grabbed the yoke and pulled back. Zelia stumbled as the ship zoomed up from the mushroom forest.

She would have ended up on her back if Talen hadn't reached out to steady her.

The ganger's grip tightened as a Genestealer appeared at the top of the viewport. It was clinging on to the hull as the voidship climbed through the planet's thin atmosphere, its claws scraping against the armourglass.

'If you've scratched my ship...' the woman told the creature, slamming the yoke to the left. The ship banked sharply sending the children tumbling to the deck.

By the time Zelia looked up, the Genestealer was gone, thrown clear by the sudden movement. The woman levelled the ship, before calling over to Mekki.

'You. Tech-Head. Can you operate cameras?'

A flash of irritation passed over Mekki's pale face. 'Of course I can.'

The woman slapped the co-pilot seat beside her. 'Then check to see if any Tyranids are still along for the ride.'

'Tyranids?' Zelia asked.

'The Genestealers,' the woman replied as Mekki slipped into the seat. 'They're a Tyranid sub-species.' Her eyes narrowed as she glanced back at Zelia. 'Don't you kids know anything?'

Zelia grabbed a chair to steady herself. 'We could start with who you are?'

The woman didn't look up from her dashboard, the ship shuddering as they broke free of the atmosphere. 'I'm the person who just saved you from a fate worse than death.'

'What's worse than death?' Talen asked.

'When it comes to Genestealers, you don't want to know.'

She turned back to her controls, which only infuriated Zelia all the more.

'Well?' she demanded.

The woman rolled her eyes. 'Fine. I'm Captain Harleen Amity and this is the *Profiteer*. Better?'

Zelia bristled at the tone, but forced

herself to remain civil. 'I'm Zelia, this is Talen and your new co-pilot is Mekki.'

'Pleased to make your acquaintance,' Amity replied. 'How are we doing with those cameras, Mekki?'

The Martian reported that the hull was clear of Genestealers, and the raucous bellow of the engines lowered in pitch to a steady thrum.

Ahead of them, the planet's atmosphere had given way to a starfield. They were back in space.

Amity thanked him, and turned towards Fleapit, who was walking around the flight deck, inquisitive eyes examining each and every station. 'And what about your furry friend?'

'That's Fleapit,' Talen said, only to be corrected by Mekki.

'Flegan-Pala,' the Martian said, using their companion's real name.

'A Jokaero,' Amity said, staring at Fleapit's orange back. 'Never seen one in the flesh. Where did you buy him?'

Fleapit turned and bared his teeth at her.

'We didn't,' Zelia said hurriedly. 'He's a survivor, like us.'

'A survivor of what?'

Zelia told the captain everything, how she and her mother had been excavating a dig on Targian when the hive world had been attacked and destroyed by invading Necrons. Zelia and the others had barely escaped with their lives.

'And you landed on a planet infested with Genestealers?' Amity whistled. 'Necrons *and* Tyranids. You must be tougher than you look. What did you say the hive world was called?'

'Targian,' Zelia repeated.

Amity shook her head. 'Can't say I've heard of it.'

She tapped one of the rings on her fingers and the flight deck lights dimmed. The air fizzed as pinpricks of light appeared around them.

'Are those stars?' Talen asked, his eyes wide.

'Top marks,' Amity replied, swatting Mekki's servo-sprite out of her way. 'This is a star map of the Imperium. Every dot represents a star system.'

She strolled through the hololith, searching every star system in turn. 'Targian... Targian... No, I can't see it.'

'It is near the Adrantis Nebula,' Mekki informed her.

Amity's eyebrows shot up. 'In the Segmentum Pacificus? But that's on the other side of the Imperium.' She twisted the ring around her finger and the holo-map zoomed in to one particular system.

'That's it,' Zelia said, recognising the fourth planet from the sun. 'That's Targian.'

'But it can't be,' Amity insisted. 'You say you escaped in a life-pod.'

Talen nodded. 'Yeah. We were thrown clear when the refugee ship made the leap into the...' He searched for the right word, his cheeks flushing as he struggled to remember.

'Into the warp?' Amity prompted.

He shifted, embarrassed. 'Yeah.'

'Talen hasn't travelled much,' Zelia cut in, trying to save the ganger's blushes. It didn't work.

'Thanks, Zelia,' he hissed.

Amity didn't seem to notice. She was shaking her head in amazement. 'You kids must have the luck of the Emperor.'

'What do you mean?' Mekki asked, rising from his seat.

Amity twisted her ring and the star chart pulled out to show the entirety of the Imperium of Mankind, over a million planets filling the bridge.

Amity strode over to a pulsing red dot near the rear of the flight deck. 'This is Targian...' she said, before pointing to a flashing yellow light by the viewport. 'And that's where I found you. A planetoid so remote it hasn't even got a name.'

A holographic line traced from one planet to the other, bisecting the map of the galaxy.

Zelia felt sick. 'But that's...'

'Impossible?' The captain walked the length of the flight deck. 'You're not joking. Somehow, you ended up in the Ultima Segmentum, travelling trillions of light years in a single bound.' She stopped in front of the pulsing yellow dot that represented the ice-planet. 'You said your ship was about to jump into the warp?'

'Could that be what did it?' Mekki asked. 'If our escape pod jettisoned at the precise moment the *Mercator* leapt into the immaterium...'

'The force propelled you from one end of the Imperium to the other?' Amity said. 'That's not how the warp works, I'm afraid. But whatever the reason, you kids are a long way from home.'

Zelia felt light-headed. She staggered, nearly losing her balance. Talen grabbed her, lowering her into an empty seat.

'Are you all right?'

She nodded, gripping hold of his arm. 'I just didn't realise how far we'd travelled. H-how far from mum we must be.'

'Your mother survived the Necron attack?'

Zelia nodded at the captain. 'Yes. She told us to meet her at the Emperor's Seat.'

Amity shrugged. 'That's a new one on me.'

'Isn't it on your space-map?' Talen asked.

The captain consulted a cogitator. 'There's nothing listed under that name.'

'It could be Terra,' Mekki suggested. Everyone turned to face the Martian. 'Where the Emperor sits on his Golden Throne,' he explained.

Amity didn't look convinced. 'Then why not just call it by its name?'

Zelia nodded. 'You're right. It has to be someplace else.'

'But where?' Talen asked, looking around at the holo-map. 'I never realised that the universe was so big.'

Zelia turned to Amity. 'Can you help us?'

The woman looked surprised. 'Me?'

'You're a rogue trader, aren't you?'

'A what?' Talen asked.

'An adventurer for hire, at least that's what Erasmus called them.'

'It's a little more complicated than that,' Amity said.

'I don't see why. Mercenaries who are given free rein to travel the galaxy, trading in the Emperor's name.'

The captain's tone hardened. 'We're not mercenaries.'

'Explorers then,' Zelia said. 'Privateers.'

'Merchants,' Amity hissed.

Zelia allowed herself to be corrected, but looked around the flight deck puzzled. 'Although I still don't understand how you fly a ship this size without a crew.'

'I have a crew,' Amity insisted, indicating the servitor still standing in the corner. 'Grunt is more useful than he looks.'

'And that is it?' asked Mekki. 'Where is your astro-navigator? Where are your technicians?'

'I work best on my own,' she snapped.

'Even through the warp?'

Amity glared at the Martian. 'How I operate my ship is none of your concern. I don't need anyone else.'

'Then, can you help us?' Zelia asked again. 'Can you help find the Emperor's Seat?'

Amity tapped her ring and the holo-chart deactivated. She strode back to her flight chair and stared out into space.

'Sorry, but I already have a mission.'

'But...'

'But nothing.' Amity busied herself with the controls. 'Look, I answered your distress call. I didn't have to, but I did. I even saved you from Genestealers, for Throne's sake. I wish I could help you with your little quest, but it's just not possible.'

'So what happens now?' Zelia asked, her shoulders slumping.

'Now you give me my reward and we part company.'

Zelia looked at her blankly. 'Your *reward*?'

'Obviously. Everything has a price, especially out here.'

'But we don't have anything,' Zelia admitted. 'Everything we owned is back on the ice-planet.'

Talen's hand went to his belt. Zelia felt a pang of sympathy for the ganger. He must have been thinking of the pouch he'd left in their abandoned camp, the pouch containing the last link he had to his family.

'I could take the Jokaero off your hands,' Amity said, nodding towards Fleapit.

The alien growled, and Amity raised her hands.

'Or maybe not.' She turned back to the flight controls. 'Look, I'll take you to the nearest planet. Maybe you can contact your mother from there.'

'What if we pay you?' Zelia asked.

Amity swivelled in her chair to face her. 'What with?'

Zelia fished the omniscope out of her bandolier and offered it to the captain. 'You can have this?'

Amity looked at it doubtfully. 'A telescope?'

'An *omniscope*,' Zelia corrected her. 'It's ancient archeotech. Probably worth a fortune.'

Amity smiled. 'Nice try, but I don't think so.' She went back to her controls, plotting in a new course.

Zelia didn't give up. 'My mum has

a hold full of this stuff, artefacts from dozens of worlds. There must be something of value. She'll pay you when we find her. Or perhaps she can cut you a deal...'

Amity looked up at that. 'What kind of deal?'

'I don't know. Erasmus used to help her sell artefacts, but now he's gone, mum will need a new business partner. An agent.'

Amity laughed. 'Do I look like an agent?'

'I don't know, but you're our last hope.' Zelia stood, walking towards the captain. 'You're right. We've been lucky so far. Really lucky, but that luck won't last forever. We need someone's help.'

Her voice caught in her throat and she fell silent.

Amity looked at each of them in turn, before glancing at the immobile servitor.

'What do you think, Grunt?'

The cyborg didn't reply.

Amity raised a hand in mock-surrender. 'Okay, okay, there's no need to go on about it.' She smiled at Zelia. 'That's the trouble with Grunt. Once you get him talking, he *never* shuts up.'

Zelia's heart skipped a beat. 'Then you'll help us? You'll find the Emperor's Seat?'

Amity turned back to her controls. 'I'm not promising anything, but I'll take you as far as Hinterland Outpost.'

'Where's that?' Talen asked.

'A trading post near Doron. I've business there anyway.'

Zelia wanted to hug the woman, but instead she tried her hardest to appear professional. 'Thank you, captain.'

'Don't thank me yet. We still don't know if this *Emperor's Seat* even exists.'

CHAPTER TWO

Hinterland

'Wow.'

Talen's eyes were as wide as storm shields as they approached the trading post. Hinterland was huge, a tumbledown space fortress built into the side of an asteroid. Crooked turrets jutted up from jagged rocks, the armoured walls pitted and cracked. Zelia didn't know if the damage had been caused by meteor strikes or energy-cannons. Either way, only Talen seemed impressed.

Amity gave the ganger a sideways look. 'Wow? *Really?*'

Zelia wanted to cut in, but knew

Talen wouldn't thank her. Up to a few weeks ago, the young ganger had never even left his hive, let alone visited a space station. The son of an Imperial Guardsman, Talen had been destined to join the Astra Militarum, but had run away from home to avoid being called up. At first, space travel had terrified him, but now his face was filled with wonder and awe.

'It's amazing,' he marvelled, staring through the viewport.

'It's a dump,' Amity said, bringing the ship to a halt. 'But it's a useful dump, full of useful people.'

'Including someone who'll know where to find the Emperor's Seat?' Zelia asked.

Amity shrugged. 'Maybe. There's one guy I know... Milon Karter. He deals in maps and information. If he doesn't know, no one will.'

She flicked open a vox-channel.

'Station master, this is Harleen Amity of the *Profiteer* requesting permission to dock.'

There was a crackle of static, before
a thin voice hissed through the
vox-casters. *'Well, well, well... look who
the gyrinx dragged in. You've got a
nerve, coming back here.'*

'Vetone,' Amity replied, ignoring the
sneer in the station master's tone. 'It's
good to hear those dulcet tones of yours
again.'

*'Wish I could say the same. You
buying or selling?'*

'Maybe a bit of both.'

'The overseer will have my hide if I

allow you to dock.'

'Do you have to tell him?'

'It depends...'

'On what?' Zelia asked.

Amity muted the conversation. 'On how much we're willing to offer as a bribe.' She reactivated the vox. 'Would three bars of Terran gold help you make up your mind?'

'No... but five would...'

Amity laughed. 'You always did strike a hard bargain. How about four?'

'Done,' came the reply. *'Just don't make me regret this.'*

'You'll hardly know we're here,' Amity told him.

A hangar door slid open to reveal a crammed landing bay.

'Proceed to berth eighteen-oh-four,' Vetone instructed her. *'And don't keep me waiting for that gold.'*

'I'll have Grunt deliver it to your quarters straight away. Amity out.'

She closed the channel, the smile dropping from her face.

'Do you have four bars of Terran gold?' asked Zelia.

Amity eased the *Profiteer* through the open doors. 'No, but we'll be long gone by the time Vetone finds out.'

The captain landed her ship with practised ease and powered down the engines. Soon they were striding through the bustling hangar bay, the sights and sounds of the trading post assaulting their senses. There were people everywhere, from cyborg dockers hauling cargo, to wounded veterans selling knick-knacks that looked like they'd fallen off the back of a transporter.

To the right of them, a bunch of spike-haired gangers huddled around a promethium drum fire, muttering to each other as if working out which ship they were going to ransack first.

Meanwhile, to the left, a group of hairy-footed Ratlings argued as they dismantled a flyer, stripping it for parts that in most cases were twice

the size of the stumpy scrappers.
There was no telling if they owned the
now-disassembled ship or not.

The air was thick with a heady mix
of sweat, engine grease and food. Zelia's
stomach rumbled, and she realised that
it had been a while since they'd eaten
anything other than ration packs. She
rifled through her pockets, searching
for anything she could use to barter
for food. She found only a few Targian
shillings, useless here – or anywhere
else, now that Targian was gone.

She turned to Talen, meaning to ask
him if he had anything to trade, but
the ganger wasn't there. She stopped
and looked around. Talen was standing
stock-still, staring at a goat-faced
Beastman who was shovelling slimy
noodles into his mouth.

Unfortunately, the abhuman had also
noticed he was being watched.

'What's your problem?' he growled.

'You're a goat,' Talen muttered.

'I'm a *what*?!' the Beastman bleated.

'Talen,' Zelia said, grabbing the ganger's arm. 'Leave the nice... man to his food.'

'But...'

'But nothing,' she hissed, pulling him away. 'What's wrong with you?'

'Did you see his face?' Talen said, still peering back at the angry spacefarer.

'Yes.'

'He was a goat.'

'Yes.'

'A goat-man.'

She sighed. 'You've seen abhumans before.'

'I've seen Ogryns,' he admitted. 'But nothing like that.' He looked embarrassed, his face colouring. 'I'm sorry, I... I'm still getting used to all this.'

Zelia looked around them, trying to imagine what it was like for Talen. Most people in the hangar bay were human, but there was a smattering of sub-species such as the stout, hairy-footed Ratlings, and the goat-faced

Beastman who was still glaring at them both with slitted eyes. Abhumans were descendants of human colonists who had mutated over thousands of years to adapt to life on alien worlds.

'I understand,' Zelia said. 'Really I do, but you can't just stare at people, especially in a place like this. It's asking for trouble. I mean, did you see the size of his horns? If he'd decided to charge at you...'

Talen nodded. 'I get it. Sorry. It won't happen again.' He glanced around, keen to change the subject. 'Where are the others?'

She didn't know. She had been so focused on getting Talen away from the Beastman that she had lost track of the rest of the group. She stood on tiptoes, trying to see above the crowd. Amity was talking to one of the Ratlings, but there was no sign of Mekki and Fleapit. Then she spotted Mekki's servo-sprite flitting around the Martian's bald head. They pushed through the crowd to find Mekki and Fleapit watching cargo being unloaded from a large cruiser.

'What's so interesting?' she asked.

The Martian pointed out the golden exo-suits that the dockers were using to lift the heavy containers, robotic arms taking the strain.

'I have never seen that design before. It reminds me of something, but I cannot tell what.'

She knew what he meant. A lot of ships carried Sentinel power-lifters, armoured walkers fitted with large claws for transporting heavy containers. The *Scriptor* had been no exception, and even Captain Amity had a couple of Sentinels in the *Profiteer*'s hold, presumably for the rare cases where Grunt needed help lifting and carrying.

But these were different. They were more like suits of armour than walkers, and just didn't match the surroundings. Everything on board the Hinterland was battered, from the ships to the workers, but the exo-suits were brand new. Whereas most Imperial lifters were crude and clunky, with hydraulic joints gushing steam and servos whining, these were sleek and near silent, barely making a sound as they went about their work.

Still, they weren't here to gawp at technology, no matter how impressive it was. Zelia was about to tell the others that they should find Captain Amity when she felt a tug at her bandolier. She put her hand to the leather belt to find her omniscope was gone. Someone had stolen it!

She whirled around to see the device in the hands of a feathered-haired Kroot. The bird-like alien was running, barging through the crowd.

'Stop,' she called out, but the thief had almost made it out of the hangar bay.

She took off after the alien, Talen racing beside her. 'Out of my way,' she cried out, slamming into the goat-faced Beastman.

The abhuman glared, making a grab for her. 'What is it with you brats?' he snarled, hairy fingers digging into her arms.

'Let me go,' Zelia spluttered, delivering a swift kick to one of his cracked hooves. The goat-man howled in pain and she wriggled free, racing out of the hangar bay to emerge onto a large market square. Stalls of all shapes and sizes stretched as far as the eye could see, selling everything from pungent fruit to cages containing critters from all across the galaxy. There were giant clams that clacked their shells in time to the music of a strange two-headed piper, and disgusting slugs with yawning mouths that, if you believed their reptilian salesmen, were perfect for squig soup. 'Just add a pinch of grox-foot,' the trader hissed, thrusting a handful of shrivelled herbs under Zelia's nose. She batted them away, getting a full whiff of their foul aroma – somewhere between ripe cheese and overboiled cabbage.

All she cared about was spotting the Kroot, but there was no sign of the yellow-skinned alien, or Talen for that matter.

She jabbed at the vox that was sewn into her tunic sleeve. 'Talen? Where are you?'

He answered straight away, breathing heavily over the link. *It got away!*

She stopped and tried to catch her breath as Mekki and Fleapit caught up with her. 'Don't worry. It doesn't matter...'

But your scope...

The thought of losing the omniscope broke her heart. She had been secretly pleased that Amity hadn't accepted it as payment. It was all she had left of her life before the Necrons.

But while her first reaction had been to chase after the thief, Zelia had to admit that running deeper into the station was a bad idea.

'Come back to the hangar bay,' she

told Talen. 'We need to find Amity.'

'*No, wait,*' came the reply. '*I can see it!*'

'Talen, don't. Kroot can be dangerous. *Really* dangerous. Please, just come back.'

But there was no answer.

'Talen? Talen, are you there?'

Zelia's stomach tightened into a knot. Talen could get really hurt if he tackled a Kroot by himself!

CHAPTER THREE

Stop, Thief!

Talen could have kicked himself.
Freaking out about an abhuman. Zelia
was right. He'd seen abhumans before,
plenty of them, but when he had
found himself standing in front of the
goat-man, with its weird yellow eyes
and curled horns, he had frozen.

He must have looked an idiot,
especially after everything that had
happened to him over the last few
weeks. Talen had been stalked by a
teleporting Necron and hung up to dry
in an Ambull's larder. He'd tackled an
angry Ogryn and escaped rampaging
Genestealers, and for what? To be fazed

by a fuzzy-faced freak eating a bowl of worm-noodles.

But there had been something unsettling about the way the abhuman sat there, doing something so mundane as eating lunch.

It just reminded him how new he was at all of this, how out of his depth.

Not any more.

This was his opportunity to prove that he could handle life in space. Catching a beak-nosed alien pickpocket on a space station shaped like a castle? Sure, why not? It wasn't like he was fighting the urge to curl up into a ball and hide.

At least the yellow thief was easy to follow. The xenos was fast on its clawed feet, but it was also tall enough to stand out among the crowd. Its mane of quills bobbed as it pelted through the throng of market-goers. Talen wasn't going to let the Kroot out of his sight, no matter what Zelia said!

The alien raced through the

marketplace, ducking into an alleyway. Talen thundered after it, nearly colliding with a critter-monger hawking a basketful of bat-snakes.

The lane was narrow, with crumbling shops on either side, the passageway covered by a cobweb-strewn ceiling. There seemed to be even more people crammed into the alley than in the market square, but Talen could still make out the Kroot's quills at the far end of the passage. He barged through the traders, not caring if he knocked them down. The Kroot darted to the left, before taking a turning to the right. Talen stayed on its tail, all too aware that he was getting lost in the labyrinthian corridors of the trading post. There was no rhyme or reason to the layout of the place. It was as if it had been designed by a madman.

They charged down yet another cramped corridor. The crowd had thinned out now, but there was no way he could catch the Kroot. Talen was fast, but the alien was faster. Talen's legs ached, and a stitch cut into his side. He was finding it hard to breathe. Soon he would have to admit defeat.

Then something caught his eye. There was a weapon stall up ahead, basic armaments racked in front of a counter. There were knives, slingshots and bo-staffs, but Talen knew exactly what he wanted. His hand flashed out as he ran past, snatching a set of bolas. He could already imagine Mekki rolling his eyes at him – *Becoming a thief to catch a thief, Talen Stormweaver?* The irony wasn't lost on him, but Talen had been a thief from the moment he joined the Warriors back on Targian. The difference here was that the feathered freak had stolen something from one of his friends. He knew how much that scope meant to Zelia. He'd lost his own link to the past when he'd been forced to leave his brother's toy Guardsman on the ice planet. There was no way he was going to let Zelia lose something just as important to her.

The stone balls clacked together as he tested the strength of the leather thongs. They could have been better, but would have to do. Ignoring the protests of the stall-holder, he started to whirl the stones above his head. His father had trained Talen in the art of combat ever since he could walk, convinced that his son would follow him into the Imperial Guard. Talen may have deserted, but the lessons had stayed with him.

The Kroot went to turn another corner.

'Oh no you don't,' Talen said, releasing the balls. The stones whistled through the air, arcing down just as Talen had planned. The alien let out a cry as the straps wrapped around its long legs. It crashed to the ground, Zelia's omniscope rolling from its grasp. Talen leapt over the alien and grabbed Zelia's prized possession. He had no idea if it was

broken, but at least the lenses seemed
intact.

Now he just had to get it back to her.

He turned, crying out as something
hard smacked into the side of his head.
Stars exploded across his vision and he
went down with a grunt.

CHAPTER FOUR

Fight

Talen groaned. He touched his forehead,
his fingers coming back slick with
blood. Whatever had struck him had
opened the old scar above his eye,
a souvenir of his initiation into the
Runak Warriors.

The Kroot loomed over him, the stolen
bolas whirling in a clawed hand. So
that's what had hit him.

The alien brought back its arm, ready
to send the stones lashing down again.
Talen rolled to his left, the heavy balls
crashing into the floor. That had nearly
been his skull!

Talen kicked out, but the alien was

ready for him. It caught his leg and swung Talen around as if he were a slab of meat. He smashed into a storefront and dropped back down to the ground, gasping for breath. He forced himself to crawl forwards and cried out in pain as the bolas slammed down onto his back.

'Dirty human cub,' the alien hissed above him. 'Teach you to mess with Korok!'

Talen couldn't get away. He could barely breathe. And yet even now, he could hear his father's voice in the back of his mind. *This is why we destroy the alien. This is why we wipe them out. It's kill or be killed, son. No concessions. No compromise.*

Korok snarled as it pulled back to deliver another blow... and was knocked flying by a ball of orange fur.

The bolas clattered to the ground, inches from Talen's aching head. He forced himself to look up. The Kroot was down, being pummelled by long arms. It was Fleapit! The Jokaero had launched himself at Korok and was punishing the Kroot, teeth bared and hairy fists flying.

'Talen!' Zelia ran up, dropping down beside him. 'You're bleeding.'

'It's nothing,' he said, pushing her hand away, never taking his eyes off the fight. Korok was reaching for the discarded bolas. Talen grabbed for the leather cords, snatching the weapon from the Kroot's reach. Korok roared in frustration and lashed out with a bony elbow, catching Fleapit in the head. Fleapit was knocked back and Korok rolled on top, pulling at the Jokaero's fur. Talen went to help, but Zelia held him back.

'Talen, don't. You'll get hurt.'

'We can't just stand by and—'

The rest of his sentence was lost as an energy bolt whizzed over them, slamming into Korok. The Kroot was thrown from Fleapit and skidded on the floor before lying still.

Talen whirled around but stumbled, suddenly dizzy. Zelia grabbed him, keeping the ganger on his feet as they stared at the human who had fired the shot.

It was a man, with a haughty expression on his lined face and a bulky beamer in his hand. He was tall and thin, wearing a silk shirt over dark trousers, his hair balding and his cheeks cavernous.

'Well, well, well,' he said, pale eyes dropping to rest on Fleapit. 'What have we here?'

'Leave him alone,' Zelia said, jumping forwards to put herself between the beamer and the Jokaero.

The man chuckled,

lowering his weapon. 'As if I would harm such a prize specimen.'

Talen felt Zelia bristle. 'He's not a specimen. He's our friend.'

The smile on the man's lips faltered. 'Careful, child. We may be on the edge of Imperial space, but there are many still loyal to the Emperor and his teachings. They won't take kindly to the suggestion that humans and aliens can be friends.'

Zelia opened her mouth but didn't get the chance to argue. Korok reared up behind them, teeth bared. The stranger's beamer flared again, hitting Korok in the shoulder. The Kroot spun on its heel before tumbling back to the ground, wailing as it clutched its wounded arm.

'See what I mean?' the man said as he brought his weapon down to point at the alien's head. 'Crawl back to where you came from, xenos. There's nothing for your kind here.'

Korok bared its teeth but scurried

away, disappearing into the crowd who had gathered to watch the fight.

The tall man returned his gaze to Zelia and Talen. 'So tell me – who are you? What are children doing on Hinterland?'

'We are with Captain Harleen Amity of the *Profiteer*,' a voice rang out behind him. The man turned to see Mekki running up to them, his servo-sprite buzzing after him.

He chuckled. 'By the Emperor. Two younglings, a Jokaero, and now...' His eyes glinted with amusement. 'What exactly are you? An initiate into the tech-priesthood?'

Mekki thrust his chin in the air. 'I am an explorator.'

The man's chuckle turned into a laugh. 'Are you now? Well, I'd heard that poor Harleen had fallen on hard times, but to employ children as her crew...'

Zelia's hands balled into fists. 'We're not her crew. We hired her.'

The man's eyebrows shot up. 'Hired her? To do what exactly? What in the name of the Throne could you want with a rogue trader of Harleen's... character?'

If Zelia heard the smirk in the man's voice, she didn't react to it. 'We're looking for one of her contacts. A man with information we require.'

'And you've found him, more's the pity.'

Amity strode up behind Mekki, her hand riding the hilt of her sword. She stopped beside the Martian, tapping the brim of her hat in greeting.

'Hello, Karter. Long time no see.'

CHAPTER FIVE

Karter

Zelia was glad to get out of the alleyways. The fight had drawn a crowd, all of whom seemed far too interested in Fleapit. Luckily, Karter was obviously a man of authority. After Amity had arrived, he'd slipped his beamer back into its holster and told the onlookers to go about their business. There had been grumbles and hangers-on, but most sloped off after Karter fixed them with a steely glare.

He'd led them back to his store, located on a busy thoroughfare. The covered street was wider than the alleyways, the shopfronts – including

Karter's own – grander than the tumbledown vendors Zelia had passed when chasing after Talen. She had no idea how Fleapit had found the ganger. Perhaps he followed Talen's scent. If so, the Jokaero's sense of smell must have been overpowered by the broth being peddled by an old woman outside Karter's emporium. The crone offered Karter a mug of her stinking slop, but the trader refused politely before unlocking the door to his premises.

The store itself was surprisingly large, the windows filled with framed parchments and star charts. As they had made their way through the outpost, Amity had explained that Karter largely dealt in cartography, selling maps both ancient and modern. However, he appeared to be a man with fingers in many different scrag-pies. The shelves and cabinets of his shop were full of antiquities and holo-cubes. Paintings hung on the walls, mostly portraits, mainly of the Emperor himself. Zelia squirmed beneath the gaze of the Immortal One, Karter's warning coming back to her.

Careful, child.

She'd felt Talen tense when Karter had advised her to hold her tongue, and knew why. Karter had been right. The message from the Golden Throne was clear: aliens weren't to be trusted. In fact, in most cases they were to be hunted down and killed. If you believed the stories, it was easy to see why. Most alien races seemed intent on slaughtering as many humans as possible. She'd seen it herself with the Necrons and Genestealers. They all had. Speaking out in support of aliens was enough to get you arrested for heresy. The penalties for deviance from the Emperor's teachings were severe.

But surely not all aliens were evil? Fleapit was an alien and he had risked his life to save them. And her mother had always taught her that violence should be avoided at all costs.

They had dug up enough weapons to know that wars had been waged for millennia. Surely humans should have learned a better way by now?

The trouble was that it had been easy to denounce weapons from the relative safety of the *Scriptor*. Out here, light years from home, things weren't so black and white. What would have happened if Karter hadn't shot the Kroot? What would have happened if Amity hadn't saved them from the Genestealers?

A cold shiver passed down Zelia's back and she hugged the omniscope to her chest. How she wished she could open the device and listen to her mum's voice.

'So,' Karter said, interrupting Zelia's thoughts, 'what information do you seek?'

The trader had perched on the edge of a large wooden counter covered in maps and quills. A curtain was pulled shut behind him, hiding what Zelia assumed was a stockroom.

'The children are looking for their parents,' Amity began, only to be cut off by Talen.

'Not me,' he said, looping his stolen bolas around his belt.

'Nor I,' Mekki added. 'My parents are dead.'

Zelia blinked. That was the first time she had ever heard the Martian speak of his family.

'And what of you, child?' Karter asked, his cold eyes focusing on Zelia.

'I am looking for my mother, yes,' she told him. 'She's an archaeologist. An explorator like Mekki.'

'Interesting,' Karter said, and indicated the various artefacts dotted around his store. 'I'm something of a collector myself. How did you get separated?'

'They were on a planet destroyed by the Necrons,' Amity said.

Karter's smile faded. 'The Necrons? That must have been... terrifying.'

It was, but Zelia wasn't about to admit

that she still had nightmares haunted by the grinning metal skeletons.

'Mum told us to meet at the Emperor's Seat.'

A flicker of recognition registered on Karter's gaunt features. 'Did she now?'

'You know where it is?'

The merchant tapped a bony knuckle against his thin lips. 'Maybe... for the right price.'

Zelia shrugged. 'I'm afraid we haven't any money.'

Karter snorted. 'Then why come to me?'

'Because you're Amity's friend.'

'Am I now?' Karter said, his eyes flicking over to Fleapit, who was examining a star chart, Mekki's servo-sprite on his shoulder. 'I wonder if you know what happens to Captain Amity's friends?'

Zelia frowned. 'What do you mean?'

'He's teasing you,' Amity said quickly, 'but I'm sure we can come to an agreement, isn't that right, Karter?'

'It depends what else you have to offer.'

'We have data,' Mekki said, tapping his wrist-screen. A hololith appeared in front of him, a flickering image of an antique reliquary. The Martian tapped the screen again, and the hololith shifted, now showing a collection of ancient helms. 'I have a record of everything we have discovered on our expeditions. A full catalogue.'

'And it can be mine if I agree to help?' Karter asked, rubbing his

fingers together. 'It is a tantalising opportunity... but no, I'm afraid not.'

Zelia's shoulders slumped.

'Have a heart, Karter,' Amity said. 'They're children.'

The cartographer fixed the captain with a curious look. 'And since when do you care about other people? Besides, have I said I won't help?'

'So you know where to find the Emperor's Seat?' Zelia asked.

'Of course I do,' Karter replied, returning his attention to her. 'Although there are at least three locations that bear that name.'

Zelia's hand tightened around the omniscope. 'What are they?'

Karter raised a skinny finger. 'All in good time, young lady. First, we must discuss terms...'

'Terms?' Talen repeated. 'We've already said we haven't any money.'

'True,' Karter agreed. 'But you do have something of value.'

Zelia realised he was looking straight

at Fleapit.

'Oh no,' she said, positioning herself in front of the Jokaero. 'No way. Fleapit isn't for sale.'

Karter smiled, showing a row of yellowing teeth. 'You've given it a name? How charming.'

'He already had one,' Mekki grumbled, stepping up to stand beside Zelia.

Talen, meanwhile, had propped himself against a statue that looked far too expensive to be used as a leaning post. 'But just to make sure we understand each other,' he said, the statue wobbling alarmingly. 'You will give us the location to the Emperor's Seat if we give you Fleapit?'

'Talen!' Zelia snapped.

'You wanted to make a deal...' Amity reminded her, but Zelia shook her head firmly.

'Not one that includes Fleapit, we don't. He stays with us.'

Karter parted his hands and rose from the counter. 'Then we have nothing to discuss. It was a pleasure to see you again, captain, but if you'd excuse me, I have much to do. You know what they say. Time is money.'

'Indeed it is,' Amity agreed, ushering the children out of the store. 'Sorry to disturb you.'

Zelia seethed as they were propelled out of the shop. They had come so close, only to be denied the information they needed. She turned, glaring at Karter through the glass door.

The cartographer still had his eyes fixed on Fleapit.

CHAPTER SIX

Old Grudges

'And that's it?' Zelia asked as they walked back through the market square. 'We're just going to give up?'

Amity led them through the crowd, never taking her hand from the hilt of her sword. 'Once Karter's mind is made up...'

'He wanted us to hand over Fleapit!' Zelia exclaimed.

The Jokaero grunted in disgust.

'We would never do that, Flegan-Pala,' Mekki assured the alien.

'There is more than one way to flog a mastodon,' Amity retorted. 'If Karter won't help us, we'll find someone who will.'

Zelia looked around at the crowd. Those who weren't staring at Fleapit in fascination were glaring openly at Amity.

'And how easy is that going to be?' Zelia asked. 'What was all that business about your friends?'

Amity stopped in her tracks to turn on Zelia.

'Listen,' she said, her voice low and dangerous. 'I don't have to do this. It's not as if you're even paying for my time. I have business of my own to attend to, so I suggest you don't try what little is left of my patience.'

Tears pricked Zelia's eyes.

'Do we understand each other?'

She nodded, unable to speak.

'Good.' The rogue trader adjusted her belt and glanced around the marketplace. 'Wait here.'

'Why?' Zelia blurted out, fighting the urge to grab Amity as she strode away.

'Where are you going?'

The captain didn't answer but strode over to a nearby hetelfish stall to strike up a conversation with the merchant.

Zelia knew what Amity was doing, leaving them alone in the middle of the crowd. It was supposed to intimidate them, to remind them how vulnerable they were in a place like this. Her skin crawled as she felt every eye in the market on her. What would they do if one of the passers-by made a grab for them? Sure, Talen could handle himself in a fight, but even he had nearly come unstuck tackling the Kroot. She might try to act tough, but inside Zelia had never been so scared in her life, and as for Mekki...

She glanced at the Martian to find him tap-tap-tapping at his screen, the servo-sprite on his shoulder, wings folded behind its back. Mekki's pale face was an expressionless mask, but a vein throbbed between the electoos on his head. He was just as frightened as she was, no matter how much he tried to distract himself with his precious data.

'Way to go, Zelia,' Talen muttered under his breath. 'Try not to get us marooned.'

She whirled on the ganger. 'I'm sorry?'

'You should be.' He jabbed a finger at the back of Amity's head. 'She's our only way off this dump. It's probably best that you don't annoy her like you annoy everyone else.'

'This dump?' Zelia parroted, crossing her arms and cocking her head. 'What happened to "wow, it's amazing"?'

Talen stepped forwards so they were almost nose to nose. 'I'll tell you what happened.' He jabbed a finger at her omniscope. 'I nearly got killed getting that thing back for you, but did you say thank you? Did you?'

Zelia's face burned. 'I never asked you to chase after it in the first place. What do you want? Another patch for your jacket. Something to show how brave you are?'

'I want some respect!' he snapped back.

Fleapit reached up to touch Talen's arm, but the ganger pulled away.

'And you can get off me!'

'He saved your life,' Mekki pointed out, looking up from his screen.

'He's a stinking alien,' Talen bellowed.

Zelia's mouth dropped open. 'I can't believe you just said that.'

From the look on his face, neither could Talen. His mouth bobbed open and shut, and he glanced at the Jokaero, who simply glared back. Talen looked away, ashamed of himself, but his expression hardened as he spotted something across the marketplace.

His nose wrinkled. 'And there's another one...'

Zelia turned to see a blue-skinned xenos standing near a stall selling animal furs. The alien was female, her head completely devoid of hair and a long slit running between her eyes where a nose should be. Her ruby eyes were narrowed and focused on Talen.

Before any of them could stop him, Talen marched towards the alien, jabbing a finger at her. 'What are you looking at?'

Another alien stepped in front of the female. He was of the same race, but at least a head taller, with a frame as powerful as the woman was slight. His bulk was only accentuated by the armour he wore under his dark robes, while his intent was clear from the three-fingered hand he placed on the sword at his waist.

Zelia looked around. More of the slit-nosed aliens had appeared in the crowd. She could count at least three – two males and another female – all equally muscled and glaring straight at Talen, who seemed oblivious to the danger he had placed himself in.

In fact, the appearance of the woman's bodyguard only seemed to rile him more.

He spread his arms, as if challenging her to a fight. 'Think you can take me, do you? Is that it? You think you can do better than the Kroot?'

Zelia caught up with him, grabbing his arm. He tried to pull away, but she wouldn't let go. 'Talen, what's got into you?'

'What's got into me? Can't you see it? They're everywhere, Zelia. Aliens. Dirty, stinking xenos.'

Sweat was beading on his forehead, his breathing shallow.

Zelia looked straight into his eyes. 'Talen, listen to me. I realise this is all new to you, but you need to calm down.'

'Calm down? How can I, with you always judging me?'

'I-I'm not.'

'Of course you are. Poor little Talen. So scared. So inexperienced. Not like you.' He turned on his heel, throwing his arms out wide to take in the entire market. 'You've seen it all before, haven't you? Zelia the galactic explorer, taking everything in her stride.'

She wasn't going to let him get away with that. She stepped up close, and let her voice drop. 'You think I'm not scared? Talen, I'm terrified. This is a *nightmare*, and I'm only just keeping it together.'

She tried to touch his hand, but he pulled away.

'Then you probably shouldn't be around me.'

He turned and walked off, fists balled at his sides.

'Talen,' Zelia called after him. 'Where are you going?'

'Just leave it, Zelia,' he called back. 'Leave me alone. Maybe dad was right all along. No concessions. No compromise.'

'What does that mean?'

A hand grabbed Zelia's shoulder. She spun around, thinking it was another thief, but it was only Amity, her conversation done.

'What's his problem?' the captain said, nodding at Talen.

'Where would you like us to start?' Mekki said flatly.

Zelia tried to gather herself. 'He's just letting off steam.'

'Then he needs to be careful,' Amity said, glancing over at the blue-skinned alien who had returned her attention to the stall, her intimidating associates having melted back into the crowd like ghosts. 'I knew this place was near the Tau Empire, but never expected to see them on the station.'

Zelia glanced at the alien. 'They're Tau?'

Amity nodded. 'At least they weren't wearing battle armour.' The captain guided Zelia towards the hangar bay. 'We should get you back to the ship.'

'What about Talen?'

'Meshwing can keep an eye on him,' Mekki told her.

Zelia's brow furrowed. 'Meshwing?'

Mekki nodded at the servo-sprite, who obediently shot into the air, zipping after Talen.

'You gave it a name?'

Mekki shrugged. 'Unless you can think of something better?'

Zelia shook her head. 'No. I like it. Meshwing it is!'

But as they walked back to the *Profiteer*, Zelia couldn't help but wonder how much help a servo-sprite would be if Talen got himself into another fight...

CHAPTER SEVEN

For the Greater Good

Zelia looked at her chrono and sighed. It had been two hours since Talen had stormed off, Meshwing bobbing after him.

The ganger still hadn't returned.

They were alone on the ship, Amity having told them not to touch anything before heading back out into the station to make further inquiries... whatever that meant. They had no idea if the captain was tracking down information about the Emperor's Seat or seeing to her own mysterious business.

Zelia didn't mind admitting that Amity made her uncomfortable. Everyone they met seemed to make jokes about the rogue trader.

And then there was her crew... or rather, the lack of one. From what Erasmus had told Zelia, rogue traders *never* worked alone. Most captains came from noble families, awarded special warrants to travel beyond Imperial borders. Some of them pushed the limits of what was right and proper, but they were usually surrounded by those who wanted to share in their riches.

Something had happened to Amity's crew, something that everyone seemed to know about. Everyone but them.

Left alone, Zelia had tried to find out more about the captain from the ship's cogitator, but unsurprisingly most of the data was encrypted. Not even Mekki could persuade the *Profiteer*'s machine-spirit to give up Amity's secrets. The Martian had admitted defeat and retreated to the ship's empty mess hall to tinker with the exo-frame that supported his withered arm.

Zelia stayed on the flight deck, accessing public files on the cogitator. She pulled up files on the Tau Empire, all too aware that Grunt was standing motionless on the far side of the bridge. The servitor wasn't even looking at her, but instead stared unblinking at the viewport like a hound waiting for its owner to return. She glanced back at the cyborg, and tried to suppress the shudder she felt every time she saw his slack expression. She knew that he wasn't real, that he had been grown in a vat, not raised as a child. Servitors were tools, nothing more, just like Mekki's servo-sprites. But she had heard a rumour a long time ago, while sitting in a tavern with her mother. A wart-faced spacefarer had been talking about his grandson, a healthy boy who had refused to go and fight in one of the Emperor's many wars.

'They turned him into one of those servitor things,' the toothless man had muttered, tears in his rheumy eyes. 'Stuck machines into him. Took away his soul.'

It was a story she'd heard a few times since, that criminals and deserters were converted into servitors, their minds wiped.

No. She couldn't believe it. Not even the Emperor would command that... would he?

Zelia tried to concentrate on the datafiles, ignoring the nagging doubts in the back of her mind. Technically, Talen was a deserter. He'd run away instead of serving in the Imperial Guard. What if he was captured and tried for his crimes? Would he end up like Grunt, standing immobile on the bridge of a spaceship?

She put the thought out of her head, focusing on what she had found in the computer.

There wasn't as much on the Tau as she'd hoped. Their empire was located on the Eastern Fringe of the galaxy, not far from Hinterland Outpost. According to one tract, the Tau believed in a philosophy they called 'the Greater Good'. They claimed that other races could voluntarily join the Empire, in order to share the Tau's superior technology. The writer of the tract obviously didn't believe them. Passage after passage had outlined the Tau's many heresies, including annexing numerous Imperial worlds and threatening to disintegrate the population unless they submitted to Tau rule.

Zelia switched off the screen and rubbed her eyes. She didn't know what to believe. The female in the market hadn't seemed threatening, not like the Kroot that had stolen her omniscope. But according to the tract, the Kroot were members of the Tau Empire. How could something so barbaric be welcomed into such a progressive and technologically advanced society? It didn't make any sense.

She glanced at her chrono again. Another half hour had passed. Trying not to look at Grunt, she got up from the terminal and went to find Mekki. Sure enough the Martian was where she had left him, still working on his frame.

'Is there any news?'

Mekki looked up, confused. 'About what?'

'About Talen,' she sighed. Who else would she be asking about?

'Ah,' Mekki said, his eyes slipping out of focus. Zelia watched his electoos flash, a sign that the Martian was communicating with Meshwing. Mekki wasn't a psyker. The link between the servo-sprite and its creator was purely artificial, a means to share raw data.

The Martian frowned.

'What is it?'

'I have lost contact with Meshwing,' he replied, looking up at her. 'This is... worrying.'

Zelia's stomach clenched. 'When did you last hear from her?'

Mekki cocked his head. 'An hour. Maybe more. I have been distracted by my work.'

'Then where's Talen?'

'Here,' said Amity, striding into the communal area. The captain had returned with Talen, who shuffled in behind her, hands thrust into his pockets.

Zelia jumped up, wanting to throw her arms around the ganger and apologise, but could tell from his face that it would be a bad idea. Instead she just asked him if he was all right.

'Of course I am,' came the gruff reply.

'It appears your friend is quite the detective,' Amity said, walking over to a decanter to pour herself a drink. The sweet tang of fortified honey filled the small room, making Zelia wrinkle her nose.

'I wouldn't go that far,' Talen muttered.

'What does Captain Amity mean?' Mekki asked.

Talen rubbed the back of his neck.
'I know where to find the Emperor's
Seat. Or at least the places that Karter
mentioned.'

Zelia clasped her hands together. 'You
found out? How?'

'Karter told me.'

'Why?' Zelia asked.

'We made a deal,' he said, refusing to
meet her gaze. 'That's all.'

A chill passed over her as she
realised what the ganger had done.
'Talen, where's Fleapit?'

The boy finally looked her in the eye,
ready for the argument he knew was
coming. 'Look, before you start—'

'Start what?' Mekki asked.

'Isn't it obvious?' Zelia snapped. 'He's
sold Fleapit.'

'What?'

Talen's face darkened. 'I got the
information, didn't I?'

'But at what cost? After everything
Fleapit has been through. After
everything he's done for us...'

'I did what we needed to do,' Talen snapped back as Mekki got to his feet, his pale face even more ashen than usual.

'The Diadem,' he said, his voice barely louder than a whisper.

'What about it?' Zelia asked.

'Flegan-Pala has it.'

Amity leant forwards in her chair, a glint of barely disguised avarice in her eyes. 'What Diadem?'

Now the colour had drained from Talen's face as well. 'But it'll be safe,'

he stammered, realising his mistake. 'It's in Fleapit's backpack thing.'

'What are you all talking about?' Amity asked, more forcibly this time.

'It's a Necron artefact,' Zelia blurted out. 'We found it on Targian.'

Now Amity was on her feet. 'It's a *what*? You brought a Necron relic on board my ship?'

'We're taking it to my mum. She'll know what to do with it.'

'Destroy it,' Amity said. 'That's what you do. You destroy it before the Necrons come looking for it.' She set her glass down, her drink half-finished. 'That's why they sent a Hunter after you.'

Zelia nodded. 'We think so, yes.'

'And that's why they'll come here. I knew answering your distress call was a mistake. I just knew it.' She was pacing up and down, trying to process the news. 'We need to warn Vetone. No... he'll never believe me. We need to find it. Find it and smash it to pieces.'

'No,' Zelia said. 'I made a promise that I'd deliver it to mum.'

Amity stopped and stared at Zelia in disbelief. 'You made a promise? Everyone on the outpost could die, but that's okay because you made a promise?'

'No. I didn't mean that. I–'

Amity covered her ears with her hands. 'I don't want to hear it. I tell you what... we're done. It's over.'

Zelia's chest tightened. 'What do you mean?'

'I mean you get off my ship, right now.'

'No,' Zelia pleaded with her. 'We can fix this.'

'Like you fixed everything else? You're children, playing at being adults. I'll send Grunt around to Karter, force him to hand back the monkey.'

'Jokaero,' Mekki chimed in.

Amity jabbed a ringed finger at the Martian. 'Not helpful.'

'And what if he won't do it? What if

85

he won't give up Fleapit?'

Amity's hand went to her beamer. 'Then, I'll just have to get the damned thing back myself.'

'No, captain, please,' Zelia begged. 'If you go in shooting, Fleapit could get hurt. Let me at least try to get him back, without servitors or guns. Then, if that doesn't work...'

Her sentence died in her throat. She didn't want to think about the alternative.

Amity stared at her, looking deep into her eyes. Zelia held her breath, half expecting the rogue trader to draw her pistol and march them off the *Profiteer.*

Instead, Amity sighed, closing her eyes and breathing heavily through her nose. 'I must be mad.' She raised a single finger. 'One hour, Zelia. You have one hour.'

'Thank you,' Zelia said, wringing her hands. 'We won't let you down. Isn't that right, Talen?'

But when Zelia looked for the ganger, he was gone.

CHAPTER EIGHT

Inquisitor Jeremias

The sleek, black ship swooped down through snow-filled clouds to land near the abandoned camp.

Jeremias of the Imperial Inquisition's Ordo Xenos strutted down the ramp, a large mechanical beast at his heels. The cyber-mastiff sniffed the cold air, an electronic growl rumbling at the back of the construct's vat-grown throat.

'What is it?' the inquisitor asked the armour-plated hound. 'The survivors?' His mouth curled into a distasteful snarl. 'Xenos?'

The mastiff's growl intensified at the accursed word. The hairs on the back of Jeremias's neck bristled. They would have to tread carefully if there were aliens here.

The inquisitor's faithful servo-skull swept down from the ship, its sensors scanning the site for evidence. The camp was deserted, a wreck of a shelter half buried in a snowdrift.

'This is intriguing,' Jeremias said as he approached the broken-down structure, his boots crunching in the snow. 'Have you ever seen the like, Corlak?' The servo-skull glided over to him, mechanical tentacles twitching.

'Nothing in records,' the skull responded in its stilted artificial voice.

Jeremias indicated the sloped walls. 'If I didn't know better, I would say the materials came from an escape pod,

but it is far too large, not to mention completely the wrong shape.'

Behind them the cyber-mastiff was churning up the snow with its snout.

'What have you found?' Jeremias asked, walking over to the hound.

The mechanical dog bit into the snow with powerful hydraulic jaws and pulled out a long metal mast, dropping the pole at its master's feet.

Jeremias bent down, probing the mast's exposed circuitry with a gloved finger and frowned. He was no tech-cultist, but even he knew that was the work of no human.

'Sire,' Corlak called over to him.

Jeremias returned to the servo-skull. There was no mistaking the claw marks his familiar had discovered. The cuts

91

were deep, made by curved talons.

'Genestealers,' Jeremias growled.

He pulled aside the section of wall, peering into the dome's interior. 'Corlak, send a report. Evidence of Tyranid infestation. Planet is to be placed under quarantine. Recommend immediate Exterminatus.'

'Complying, sire.'

Telling the skull to wait outside, Jeremias stepped into the dome, having to stoop to stand beneath the partially collapsed roof. A pouch lay in the middle of the shelter. Jeremias crouched down to pick it up, noticing the Munitorum stamp on the leather.

'Property of the Imperial Guard. Fascinating.'

He stood, flipping open the pouch. It was empty, save for a small wooden figure. A Guardsman, crouched on one knee, lasrifle extended.

A child's toy.

Removing one of his gloves, he dropped the figure into his palm, curling his fingers around the soldier.

Concentrating, he closed his eyes and waited for the images to flood his mind. When they came, they took his breath away, discordant memories that weren't his own.

Emerald lightning, crackling through the sky.

A mighty hive crashing down into the ground. Clouds of dust billowing out across a poisoned landscape.

Ships ripped apart. Ships full of survivors. Of refugees.

Then, fear. Fear unlike anything he'd experienced before.

An escape pod flung across the stars.

Impossible lights squirming through the void.

A crash, the pod rolling over and over.

Being chased through a forest, cold fingers grasping for his flesh.

The sound of a disintegrator cannon.

A rictus grin.

A ring of metal etched with strange inhuman glyphs.

Jeremias let out a ragged breath and lurched forwards. Corlak shot into the shelter, telescopic fronds ready to assist. Jeremias raised a shaking hand. 'All is well.'

Outside the ramshackle dome, the cyber-mastiff growled.

Jeremias locked eyes with the hound, all too aware that the beast had hunched its powerful shoulders and was ready to pounce.

'Heel,' he warned, ignoring the squirming sensation at the back of his mind. It was always the same when he used his powers, each experience more unsettling than the last.

The hound snarled, but its sprung limbs relaxed.

Jeremias returned the figurine to the pouch and staggered out of the dome. He passed the bag to Corlak and pulled on his glove.

His mind raced as he marched back to his ship, the hound skulking behind him.

Now he knew who they were looking for, faces glimpsed in the maelstrom of images that had invaded his mind.

A dark-skinned girl, a blond-haired boy and a pale-skinned Martian.

Children. Lost and alone. Jeremias imagined how scared they would be, how vulnerable.

As the ship took off, Corlak at the controls, Jeremias sank back into his command chair.

'Help me find them, Emperor of Mankind,' he muttered, hands clasped around his Inquisitorial seal. 'Help me find them before it is too late.'

CHAPTER NINE

Abominable Intelligence

Hinterland's marketplace seemed busier than ever. The lume-globes in the arched ceilings had dimmed to plunge the station into an artificial night, but no one seemed to be heading for bed. The atmosphere seemed charged, somehow even more dangerous.

Zelia clutched her omniscope to her, just in case another opportunist took a fancy to the device. Mekki stayed close as they made their way through the stalls and she wondered if he felt the same. Like they were being watched.

They passed a tavern, harsh music filtering through the flimsy swing doors.

Someone was hammering out a raucous star shanty on a synthi-chord, drunken patrons singing along with gusto, whether they could follow the tune or not.

'Hey hey, little ones,' a gruff voice rang out from the shadows. 'The market's no place for you, not at this time of night. Come in. Warm your hands by the brazier. We'll protect you.'

Mekki hesitated and for one awful moment, Zelia thought he was going to take the heckler up on the offer. She grabbed his arm, and pulled him away from the grog-house.

'Your loss, little ones,' the voice shouted after them. 'Stay safe, won't ya?'

Zelia shuddered. She wished Talen was with them. Yes, she was still furious with him, but at least she felt safer when he was around.

Something small and bronze darted towards them. She ducked, before recognising the whirr of tiny wings.

Mekki's servo-sprite bobbed in the air in front of them.

'Oh, look who it is,' she said, scolding the construct, as if it was an errant child. 'Where were you when Fleapit needed help?'

Mekki cocked his head, his electoos flaring as he received information from the skittish robot. 'You cannot blame Meshwing. Talen Stormweaver has spent years evading capture. If he managed to evade the Imperial Guard on Targian–'

Zelia sighed. 'Losing a servo-sprite on a busy space station wouldn't be much of an issue. I know, I know.'

She carried on, not wanting to linger in the marketplace. They hurried through the square, heading into the maze of alleyways that led to Karter's store.

It was even gloomier in the narrow passageways, steam rising from grates in the floor. Beggars huddled around broken thermo-heaters, holding out emaciated hands as they passed, but Zelia had nothing to give.

Thankfully, Meshwing could remember the way. The sprite flew ahead, leading them back to Karter's emporium. The old woman still stood outside the cartographer's door, selling her mugs of scuzzy broth.

Zelia pushed open the door to find the shop empty, lit only by flickering candles set on floating repulsor-pads.

Her first instinct was to call out, but she held her tongue. The curtain at the back of the store was drawn back slightly, a warm glow coming from behind the thick fabric.

Zelia indicated for Mekki to follow her and they crept towards the curtain, the whirr of the servo-sprite's wings ridiculously loud in the quiet shop.

Zelia had been right. The curtain did hide a stockroom. Wooden shelving units reached up to the ceiling, filled with piles of rolled-up scrolls and tiny caskets. A large metal barrel stood at the back of the narrow space. It was almost as tall as Zelia, with a heavy lid. Wanting a closer look, she reached out to pull back a curtain.

'Halt!'

Zelia jumped back as a large disc-shaped machine appeared from behind the drape. It hovered in front of them, their shocked faces reflecting in its dark picter-lens.

The machine darted forwards, forcing Zelia to step back. She whacked into the counter, yelping as her back made contact with the map-covered table.

'You are not permitted,' the hovering robot announced, its artificial tone decidedly hostile. 'The shop is closed.'

'I'm sorry,' she stammered in reply, staring into the lens. 'We're looking for Karter.'

'Not permitted,' the machine repeated, a tapered tube clicking down beside the lens. Was that a laser?

'We can come back later,' she said, trying to get out from behind the counter, but the machine bobbed forwards, blocking her path. 'Please. We didn't mean any harm.'

'Trespassers will be disintegrated.'

'What? That's a bit extreme!'

The tip of the laser glowed.

'Meshwing, go!' Mekki shouted, and the servo-sprite threw itself in front of Zelia before the defensive drone could fire.

'Out of my way,' the robot barked as Meshwing flitted back and forth to block its aim.

It was the distraction Zelia needed.

Sweeping her arm over the counter, she threw a pile of parchments over the befuddled robot.

Scrabbling over the counter, she bolted for the exit, only sliding to a halt when the door suddenly opened.

'What are you doing here?' snapped Karter, a mug of steaming broth in his hand.

The drone zipped forwards, its laser glowing ominously.

'They are thieves,' it reported, aiming straight at Zelia. 'They must be punished.'

'No,' Zelia insisted. 'We didn't take anything.'

The drone spun around to face her. 'Then why were you skulking around in the dark?'

Karter stepped into his shop, shutting the door behind him. 'That's a good point.'

'Thank you,' said the drone.

'We want Fleapit,' Zelia told the merchant.

'Your Jokaero?'

'Our *friend*.'

Karter laughed, only stopping to blow into the mug to cool his drink. 'What did I warn you about such heresies, my dear? Aliens and humans can never be friends.'

'You want to talk about heresy?' Zelia said, pointing at the hovering robot. 'What about that thing?'

Karter glanced at the floating machine. 'My drone?'

'It talks...' Mekki chipped in from behind Zelia. 'It *reasons*.'

'What of it?' bristled the drone.

'See?' Mekki said.

Karter took a sip of the broth. 'The drone is a tool, nothing more.' His eyes settled on Meshwing, fluttering near Mekki's head. 'Much like your own... creation.'

Mekki bristled at the accusation. 'It is nothing like my servo-sprite. Meshwing is not sentient, but your drone thinks for itself. It is an abomination.'

'What if we reported you to the station master?' Zelia asked, drawing another chuckle from the cartographer.

'Be my guest.'

Zelia shifted uneasily. She hadn't expected the man to call her bluff.

'And while they are here,' Karter continued, 'you can explain why you tried to steal something that is rightfully mine.'

'That's a lie!'

Karter raised an eyebrow. 'Is it? I made a deal with your ganger-friend. I gave him the information you sought, and he gave me the Jokaero. And what did you do? You broke into my store and vandalised my property.'

'The door was open,' Mekki insisted. 'And we did not touch anything.'

'Really?' Karter said, nodding towards the papers scattered on the floor beside the counter. 'You're lucky I don't make you pay for the damage. Now get out, before I let my drone open fire.'

Zelia considered knocking that

stinking mug of broth out of Karter's gnarled hand, imagining it splashing up into his smug face. But she knew it wouldn't do any good. The drone would shoot them before they had a chance to escape. Instead she forced herself to apologise and told Mekki that they should get back to the ship.

Karter stepped aside and opened the door. 'Thanks for dropping by,' he said as Zelia stepped out into the alleyway. 'Please make sure it never happens again.'

The door slammed shut behind them. There was a sharp click as Karter threw the lock. The drone glared at them through the window for a moment, before retreating into the shadows.

Zelia felt like screaming.

'Do not worry,' Mekki said, leading her away from the shop. 'We will recover Flegan-Pala.'

'How?' she replied, stopping to glare at Karter's window display. 'Karter will never let us back in now.'

'He will not have to,' the Martian told her. He pointed to the window, and Zelia saw what looked like a small figurine standing immobile among Karter's wares.

A figurine with fragile golden wings.

'That's Meshwing.'

'She hid while Karter threatened you,' Mekki explained. 'We shall wait until the cartographer has left for the night...'

'And then Meshwing will let us in.'

'Exactly.'

'But what about the drone?'

Mekki looked back at the shop door. 'It took me by surprise when it first appeared, but I will search my database. There must be something in your mother's notes that can help me deactivate that abomination once and for all.'

Zelia grinned at her friend.

'You're brilliant, do you know that, Mekki? Absolutely brilliant.'

The Martian considered this for a moment. 'Yes,' he finally agreed. 'Yes I am.'

CHAPTER TEN

Ambushed

Zelia and Mekki headed back for
Amity's ship, only to find the *Profiteer*'s
ramp was raised.

Zelia tapped her vox. 'Er, Amity? Are
you there? Captain?'

There was no response.

'Little humans... all locked out...'
squawked a voice from nearby.

They turned to see a group of
aliens emerging from the shadows of
a neighbouring ship. Zelia swallowed,
wanting to grab Mekki's hand.

It was Korok, the Kroot who had
stolen her omniscope. Now armed with
a long, hooked staff, the yellow-skinned

alien had recovered from Karter's shot and this time wasn't alone.

Another Kroot stood to its right, this one even taller, its height accentuated by the spiked mohican that ran the length of its scarred scalp. It was holding back a creature on a thick chain, a snarling monstrosity of a hound that looked like a cross between a Kroot and a wild dog, a mane of spines covering its back. Foam flecked the brute's jaws, its yellow lips drawn back to reveal teeth that looked as

though they could crunch through ceramite.

Then there was the goat-faced abhuman that Talen had insulted while he ate his lunch. The noodles were gone, replaced by a double-barrelled lasrifle. The Beastman snorted, nostrils flaring as he disengaged the weapon's safety catch.

The gang was completed by a docker encased in one of the powerful exo-suits that had so fascinated Mekki on their arrival. Zelia realised that the suit was the same gold as Karter's drone, strange glyphs running along its powerful arms.

'That's mine,' Korok said, jabbing its finger at the omniscope, now safely stowed in Zelia's bandolier.

'No, it's not,' she said, hoping the alien couldn't hear the quaver in her voice.

Korok snorted, and glanced up at the *Profiteer*. 'Nice ship, too... Amity's ship.' Its scarred beak peeled back into a hideous smile. '*My* ship now.'

'Leave us alone,' Mekki said, sounding calmer than Zelia felt. 'Captain Amity is with us.'

The gang of louts looked around. 'Funny,' scoffed the goat-man. 'I don't see her.'

Korok tapped its shoulder. The skin was blistered and raw. 'Beam hurt. Now you hurt too.'

'But that wasn't us,' Zelia argued, trying not to look at the Kroot hound that strained against its leash. 'That was Karter.'

The Kroot's spines bristled. 'Karter's my friend. You a stranger. That means you get hurt first.'

Zelia and Mekki did the only thing they could. They ran, ducking beneath the *Profiteer*.

'Split up,' Zelia yelled, peeling off to the left. Mekki darted to the right, as Korok shouted at its compatriot to release the hound.

Zelia didn't look back. She didn't have

to. She could hear the savage barking as the beast bounded after her.

She ran towards a planet-hopper, not unlike her mother's ship, with the same ladder leading up to its roof. She leapt for the bottom rung, hauling herself up. The hound leapt up after her, its snapping jaws narrowly missing her foot. She didn't look down, the rust on the rungs cutting into her palms as she climbed. The beast barked furiously beneath her, but she was safe. There was no way the animal could climb after her.

A bolt of energy slammed into the hull beside her, nearly knocking her from the ladder. She glanced over her shoulder to see Korok and the goat-man running for the planet-hopper. Both were firing, the Kroot's staff doubling as a gun. Las-fire strafed the side of the ship as Zelia threw herself onto the squat craft's roof, ducking behind a large communication disc. The bolts sounded even louder as they slammed into her makeshift shield.

Out of the corner of her eye she spotted Mekki, hiding behind a stack of cargo pods. Not that it did him any good. The docker in the exo-suit lumbered up and took out the entire pile with a single swing of her armoured arms. Mekki scuttled away, the docker trudging after the Martian, before an energy bolt struck her right between the armoured shoulders. Sparks erupted from the back of the suit, the hydraulic limbs going stiff. With a cry, the docker tumbled forwards, her armour completely immobilised.

Korok and the Beastman spun around, firing back towards the *Profiteer*. The Kroot hound gave up on Zelia and charged towards Amity's ship, barking wildly. It screeched to a halt as a silver ball dropped in front of it. The canister bounced once before rolling to the hound's feet. The beast sniffed it and then yelped as the canister detonated, a pulse of brilliant white light washing over the hangar bay.

Zelia fell back on the top of the planet-hopper, unable to see. She rubbed furiously at her aching eyes as the sounds of beamer fire filled the bay. Zelia kept her head down, blinking until her vision returned. When she finally looked up, the hangar was ominously silent.

Zelia scrambled forwards, peering over the edge of the ship to see Korok lying in a heap on the floor. There was no sign of the Beastman, although the docker still lay immobile on her front, smoke curling up from the suit's servos.

There was a sound like someone dragging a slab of meat, and Grunt emerged from beneath the *Profiteer*. The servitor was lugging the mohawked Kroot behind him. Without a word, the giant dropped the alien's prone body next to Korok and turned to watch his mistress stroll towards them. Amity had her sword in one hand and her beamer in the other. Her usually immaculate hair fell around her shoulders and, even though she was breathing heavily, there was no mistaking the swagger in her step.

'You can come down now,' she called up to Zelia.

'But that hound...'

'Ran off with its tail between its legs.'

Zelia clambered down the ladder, joining Amity beside the unconscious Kroot.

'Are they...?' She didn't want to finish the sentence.

'You won't have to worry about them any more,' Amity said, slipping her beamer back into its holster. 'Although you're lucky we came back when we did. I always find it's best to return fire if someone's trying to atomise you.'

'Zelia Lor does not carry weapons,' Mekki informed the captain, emerging from his hiding place.

'Then it's a wonder Zelia Lor is still alive,' Amity said, returning her sword to its scabbard. 'Looks like we need a lesson in self-defence.'

She led them onto the *Profiteer*, taking them not to the flight deck, but the ship's extensive armoury. The walls were covered in racks containing all kinds of weapons, from powerblades to vibro-lashes. Zelia felt a pang of regret when she realised how Talen's eyes would have popped out on stalks if he could see all this. He should be here, with them.

'Here,' said Amity, plucking a silver canister from a case. It was the same as the device that had blinded the Kroot hound. 'Stick this in your belt.'

Zelia hesitated and Amity rolled her eyes.

'It's just a flash grenade. Non-lethal, but you saw what it can do. Lots of light...'

'Hence the name,' Zelia said.

Amity nodded. 'If you get into trouble,

twist the canister to prime the flare and throw it to the ground.'

Zelia took the silver sphere gingerly, as if the device would explode at any moment, then slipped it into a spare pouch on her bandolier. Amity passed her two more. 'Just make sure you close your eyes first.'

The captain turned to Mekki. 'What about you, Tech-Head? Take your pick.'

The Martian strolled up and down the weapon bays, before retrieving a long, wand-like device. It had a power pack at one end and forked prongs at the other. Amity nodded in appreciation. 'A shock-prod. Not a bad choice, although you'll have to be up close and personal for it to work. Have neither of you really handled a weapon before?'

'I have,' Mekki said, drawing a shocked glance from Zelia.

'When?'

He slipped the prod into a pocket on his backpack. 'Long before I met your mother. When I esc–' He paused, that nerve pulsing between his electoos again. 'I mean, when I left Mars.'

Once again, Zelia realised how little she knew about the Martian, but this wasn't the time for more questions.

Satisfied, Amity ushered them out of the armoury.

'So, what happened with your Jokaero? I'm assuming that Karter didn't want to return the merchandise.'

Zelia and Mekki followed her back to the bridge, Grunt lumbering behind.

'No,' Zelia admitted. 'He said he

bought him fair and square.'

'And your ganger friend?' Amity asked, fastening her hair in a ponytail as she strode onto the flight deck.

Zelia shook her head. 'I've no idea where Talen is.'

The captain took a deep breath. 'Then, I guess it's down to me.'

'What do you mean?' Zelia asked, as Amity checked the charge on her beamer.

'I still have business of my own to attend to, but after I'm done, I'll swing by Karter's. Maybe I can *persuade* him to change his mind.'

Amity returned the gun to her belt and recovered her hat from Grunt's head.

'Protect the children,' she told the servitor. 'Nothing bad happens to them. Do you understand?'

Grunt's head jerked forwards in a rough approximation of a nod, and Amity slapped the servitor on its metal arm.

'Excellent.' She swept from the bridge, telling Zelia and Mekki to stay on the ship until she returned.

Once they were alone, Mekki started checking his wrist-screen.

'What are you doing?' Zelia asked.

'Looking for mentions of thinking drones.'

'Like Karter's?'

Mekki nodded, although it soon became clear that his database contained nothing that could help. He moved to a nearby console, slipping his haptic implants into an access port, and consulted the ship's own computer banks.

'Anything?' Zelia asked, but Mekki shook his head.

'I am afraid not. Of course, any information on Abominable Intelligence would probably have been expunged from the records.' The Martian's face darkened. 'I should have thought of that.'

Zelia couldn't let him get maudlin.

'We'll just have to improvise.' She turned to leave. 'Come on. Karter must have left by now.'

The Martian hesitated.

'What is it?' Zelia asked.

'The captain told us to stay on board the ship.'

'She works for us,' Zelia reminded him, 'not the other way around.'

'But the drone...' Mekki said, as Zelia went to leave. 'I still do not know how to deactivate it. Perhaps it is better if we leave it to Captain Amity.'

Zelia shook her head. 'If Amity goes in guns blazing, there's a chance that Fleapit could get hurt.' Then she turned to Grunt. 'Amity told you to protect us, right?'

The servitor nodded.

'So that means that if we leave the ship, you have to come with us, yes?'

Again, Grunt nodded.

Zelia grinned at Mekki. 'See? We have our very own bodyguard.'

Mekki rose from his seat, grabbing

the shock-prod from his backpack. 'Then what are we waiting for, Zelia Lor? We must rescue Flegan-Pala.'

CHAPTER ELEVEN

Breaking and Entering

The trading post had at last quietened down by the time they crossed the market square. The taverns were finally closed and the alleyways deserted. Only a few stragglers remained at large, Ratlings staggering home to wherever they lay their hairy heads, while dock workers slumped in dark corners, coats pulled over them like blankets. The stalls were now empty, the interior of the station unnaturally quiet without the bustle of the spacefarers and the barks and growls of the caged animals. Somewhere in the distance, a lone beast howled. Zelia tried not to imagine what it was, her mind conjuring up images of clawed fiends lurking around every corner, waiting to pounce upon anyone foolish enough to venture out during the outpost's night cycle.

Before leaving the ship, Zelia had found a couple of dark green cloaks in the empty crew quarters. Passing one to Mekki, she had wrapped the thick cape around her and headed out into the hangar bay. She hadn't bothered giving one to Grunt, thinking that a servitor wearing a cloak would only attract attention.

They slipped unnoticed through the market, even with Grunt plodding after them.

The broth-seller was gone by the time they reached Karter's emporium. The store was in darkness, Meshwing still standing like a tiny bronze statue in the window. Mekki tapped on the glass, and the servo-sprite snapped back to life. It buzzed excitedly over to the door and, with a sharp click, turned the lock.

The door creaked as Zelia pushed it open, and she half expected the drone to come zipping out at them. But Meshwing reported that both Karter and the drone had left the store some time ago. They could search for Fleapit in peace.

She held the door open for Grunt, who clunked his head on the frame. Mekki was already making for the stockroom as she locked them in.

A thud from beyond the curtain stopped him in his tracks. The Martian froze, looking back at her. Maybe Meshwing had been wrong? Perhaps the drone was still lying in wait for would-be thieves?

Zelia reached beneath her cloak, her fingers finding one of the flash grenades nestled in her bandolier.

Indicating for the others to stay quiet, she crept forwards, wincing as Grunt followed anyway, every step as light and airy as a ten-tonne crotalid.

Zelia tiptoed around the counter and reached for the drape. She waited for Grunt to trudge to a halt behind her and yanked the fabric back, its hoops squealing on the brass pole.

The stockroom was empty. No Karter, and no drone.

Stepping around her, Mekki activated the lume-bead he wore on the band around his head. He moved inside the storage room, the light sweeping across the shelves as he turned his head.

Zelia followed him in, leaving Grunt standing guard at the threshold. She peered at the dusty boxes on the shelves, her curiosity getting the better of her. Yellowing labels described the content of each casket in what she assumed was Karter's spidery handwriting. There were relics and old coins, quills and bottles of ink, none of which interested her, but the maps were something else. She ran her fingers along the fragile rolls of paper, wondering if any of them contained the location of the Emperor's Seat, knowledge that Talen now possessed but had failed to share before storming off.

Her eyes rested on the large barrel at the back of the room. She moved over to examine it, but froze when the front door rattled.

Zelia dashed back to the curtain, and barked for Grunt to get out of the way so she could pull it shut. They listened as the lock turned, and the shop door creaked open. The glow from Mekki's lume-bead cast stark shadows against

the curtain and she waved at him
to extinguish the light before it gave
them away. He obliged, plunging the
stockroom into near darkness.

Zelia pulled a flash grenade from her
belt as Mekki drew his shock-prod.
Even Grunt shifted behind them, ready
to protect his young charges. Zelia put
a hand against the servitor's chest to
stop him from blundering forwards,
wincing at the feel of his skin beneath
her palm. Grunt's flesh was cold and
clammy. It was like touching a dead
fish. She pulled her hand away, but
Grunt remained where he was, waiting
and watching from beneath his heavy
brow.

Footsteps rang out on the other side
of the curtain. Was it Karter? Zelia
listened for the telltale hum of the
drone, but could only hear boots pacing
the shop. They stopped, and there was
a scrape as an item was removed from
one of Karter's displays, only to be
replaced a few seconds later.

And then, there was silence.

Zelia raised a shaking finger to her lips. Mekki nodded, his knuckles white around the shock-prod. None of them moved, not even Meshwing, who cringed on Mekki's shoulder, wings folded behind her metal back.

Zelia held her breath. Any sound could betray them.

Something inside the metal barrel clanged.

Zelia couldn't help but let out a yelp. The footsteps approached, attracted by the noise. Zelia stepped back, hiding behind Grunt's bulk. Her cloak slipped from her shoulders, the flash grenade in her hand.

The footsteps stopped on the other side of the curtain. Zelia looked down to see polished boots in the gap beneath the fabric. There was an agonising wait and then with a dramatic *swish,* the drape was pulled back.

Grunt lurched forwards, but stopped

short when he found himself staring into the barrel of Captain Amity's beamer.

Zelia let out a breath of relief.

'I thought I told you to stay on the ship,' Amity snapped, returning her pistol to her belt.

'And we ignored you,' Zelia said, holstering her grenade. Only Mekki still held out his weapon, just in case, the shock-prod shaking ever so slightly in his grip.

Amity reached out and lowered the Martian's hand.

'Breaking and entering, eh?' A smile spread across the captain's face. 'Just what I would have done.'

'What you *did*,' Zelia corrected her. 'What are you doing here?'

She looked around the stockroom. 'Same as you – searching for our furry friend. Any luck?'

Zelia pointed out the barrel. 'There's something in there.'

Sure enough, another thud came from

within the container.

'It's certainly large enough,' Amity said, stepping past Grunt to try the lid. It wouldn't budge.

'How are we going to open it?' asked Zelia.

'The same way I opened the front door,' Amity replied, delving into one of the pockets in her coat. She pulled out a small box the size of a large beetle and slapped it onto the side of the barrel. It magna-locked into place and started to whine the moment she pulled back her hand.

Mekki looked on in fascination. Amity flashed him a grin.

'Sonic pick,' she explained. 'Never found a lock it couldn't open. Aha!'

There was a mechanical click from within the barrel and the container shook violently. Amity took a step back. They all did. There was definitely something inside.

'Fleapit?' Zelia asked, as the top of the barrel started to unscrew by itself.

'You might want to get ready with that shock-prod,' Amity told Mekki, drawing her beamer.

Zelia reached out a hand to calm them. 'It'll be all right. He's probably just scared.'

Mekki nodded. 'Flegan-Pala hates being locked up.'

Amity aimed her beamer at the slowly revolving lid. 'How do we know that he's in there?'

'Who else would it be?' Zelia asked as the lid stopped turning and shot up into the air.

Something burst from the barrel with a roar. Something that definitely wasn't Fleapit!

CHAPTER TWELVE

The Thing in the Barrel

The barrel toppled onto its side, briny water slopping all over the floor. But it wasn't the water gushing from the open container that worried Zelia; it was the squirming mass of tentacles.

She dropped to the floor as a suckered arm swept over her. She tried to scramble back to her feet, slipping on the water as another rubbery limb almost took out Mekki.

None of this made sense.

How had something this big fitted into a barrel that small? Zelia counted six, seven, maybe even eight tentacles flailing around the small room. There was no way they could have all crammed into the barrel and yet more seemed to spill out of the open lid with every passing second.

To make things worse, each tentacle ended in a barbed claw. Zelia screamed as one of the curved hooks slashed down towards her. She rolled, the tip smashing into the floor inches from her head.

She looked up to see a blubbery body squeezing out of the barrel. It was covered in eyes, its gaping maw filled with row upon row of glistening fangs.

Amity pulled out her beamer and fired into the mouth of the beast. Zelia ducked as another tentacle swiped towards her. She reached out, grabbing the edge of her drenched cloak. Twisting, she whipped the soaked cape at the claw, the fabric catching on the barbs. The tentacle jerked back, lifting Zelia from the floor. She let go, slamming back down, winding herself. The claw slashed down again, the now-tattered cloak still attached to its hooks. Zelia threw up a hand to protect herself, but the tentacle was sliced in two by Amity's whirling sword.

The severed claw clattered to the floor beside Zelia as the monster bellowed in agony. The noise was unbearable. Zelia clamped her hands over her ears, only to feel the severed tentacle snaking around her body. It plucked her from the ground, immediately tightening around her chest. She yelled for help, hoping another swipe from Amity's blade would cut her free, but the captain was busy fighting a suckered arm of her own.

The monster's grip tightened, crushing the breath from her lungs. She squirmed, trying to wriggle free, but it was no good. She couldn't breathe. She couldn't even scream.

Her head started to swim, black dots dancing on the edge of her vision. Then something slammed into the feeler's slimy flesh. It was Grunt, swinging his mechanical arm like a cudgel. The servitor was still trying to obey the order to protect Zelia from harm. Some hope. Another tentacle unfurled, smashing Grunt into the wall. The servitor tumbled forwards, and a heavy wooden shelf crashed down on top of him, Karter's precious stock smashing on the slick floor. Zelia yelled his name, but Grunt lay still.

She was on her own. Gritting her teeth, Zelia pushed her hand past the suckers that were pressed against her body. Her fingers curled around one of the flash grenades and, gasping for air, she threw it behind her. The device detonated, bathing the room in dazzling light. The creature roared, throwing Zelia clear. She smacked into the wall, sliding down to land on something hard. She felt beneath herself, realising that it was Amity's beamer. She pulled out the weapon, her vision clearing to see both the captain and Mekki being dragged towards the creature's open mouth.

'What are you waiting for?' Amity yelled. 'Shoot it!'

Zelia raised the gun. It felt weird in her hands. She had promised herself she would never fire a beamer, but her friends would die if she didn't act fast.

She raised the weapon, aiming straight for the monster.

Amity was clawing at the floor, trying to stop herself being pulled into the thing's mouth. Zelia's finger curled around the trigger and–

Vzzzzzzzt!

Electricity danced over the monster's body, illuminating each sucker-strewn tentacle.

But Zelia hadn't fired...

She looked down to see Mekki on the floor. He was lying face down, his arm extended, shock-prod in his hand. He'd electrocuted the creature, the charge surging through the briny water. The beast had slumped to the ground, the mighty tentacles curled around its body. Zelia ran to Mekki, trying to pull him

up. His robes were wet through. He
had been lying in the water himself.

'Mekki?'

Zelia turned him over. His eyes were
closed, his lips parted.

'Mekki!'

The Martian's eyelids flicked open. He
looked up at her, green eyes swimming
into focus. 'Did it work?' he croaked.

The monster shuddered but lay still.

'Yes,' she said, helping him up, 'but
there's no telling how long that thing
will be out. I thought you were–'

'You need to have more faith, Zelia Lor,' Mekki said, cutting her off. He was back on his feet, but swaying. 'I used my electoos to divert the charge into my pack's batteries. I was quite safe.'

'Glad one of us was,' Amity said, kicking her ankle free from the stunned creature's grip. Her hair was standing on end and her teeth chattered as she tried to stand, before slumping back to her knees. She must have taken quite a blast herself.

Zelia moved to help her up, but she pushed her away, staggering over to check on Grunt. 'He'll be okay,' Amity said. 'But we might have to carry him back to the ship.'

'We still need to find Fleapit,' Zelia reminded her, keeping one eye on the twitching creature.

Amity grabbed her beamer and went to retrieve her sword, nearly slipping on the floor. 'You never give up, do you?'

But before Zelia could answer, a voice rang out from the front of the shop.

'What in the Emperor's name is going on?'

Zelia looked past the curtain to see Karter glaring at them, the golden drone floating by his side.

CHAPTER THIRTEEN

Firing Squad

Amity snapped her gun arm up, the hovering drone in her sights.

'I could ask you the same question. Who keeps a monster inside a barrel?'

Karter rushed forwards, barging past the captain to stare in disbelief at the unconscious creature.

'What is it?' Zelia gasped.

'A kraken hatchling,' Karter replied, wringing his hands together. 'Part of a consignment from one of the finest xenos hunters in the galaxy. If you've hurt it...'

'If we hurt *it*?' Amity said. 'What possessed you to start dealing in *krakens*?'

Karter cautiously approached the monster. 'I have contacts who pay a small fortune for such beasts.'

Zelia couldn't believe what she was hearing. 'Why would anyone want something like *that*?'

The cartographer glared at her. 'How am I supposed to know? Perhaps they have strange taste in pets, or need a way to dispose of meddling children? Either way, they're not the kind of people you question.' The merchant glanced back at the drone. 'We need to administer a sedative, although squeezing it back into the stasis-barrel isn't going to be fun.'

The drone whizzed into the stockroom and dipped down in front of the creature. It extended a syringe, which was immediately shattered into a thousand pieces by a well-aimed blast from Amity's beamer. Karter and the drone whirled around, its laser ready to return fire.

'What do you think you're doing?'

Karter spluttered. 'If the monster wakes up...'

'You'll have a problem on your hands,' Amity said calmly. 'Move another muscle and I'll destroy that flying contraption of yours.'

'The kraken could kill us...' Karter pleaded.

'It already tried.'

'You're making a big mistake,' the cartographer snarled at the captain.

'Am I? You have a choice, Karter. Tell my young friends where to find the Jokaero or I destroy your drone. I'd like to see you tackle a kraken without it.'

'That's blackmail,' Karter spat.

'Yes,' Amity agreed. 'Yes, it is. And there's more where that came from. Mekki, have you been recording all this?'

'Of course,' the Martian replied.

Karter laughed bitterly. 'And I suppose you'll carry out the young lady's threat, and report me to the authorities.'

Amity considered this. 'Selling alien

livestock without a licence, and having a Tau drone at your beck and call? I may not have many friends these days, but I know a few inquisitors who would find your little operation particularly fascinating.'

'You wouldn't,' Karter said, his face blanching at the mere mention of the Inquisition.

'Try me,' Amity said as the kraken let out a groan, its long limbs twitching. The creature was stirring.

'Oh, very well,' Karter snapped. 'But you won't find the Jokaero here. I've already sold him.'

Zelia's heart leapt to her mouth. 'To who?'

Karter opened his mouth to reply, but was gagged as a suckered arm wrapped around his face. His eyes went wide as he was pulled back into the now-very-awake kraken's mouth.

The creature swallowed the merchant in one gigantic gulp.

'Master!' the drone yelled, emptying its

multi-las into the kraken. The monster
responded by grabbing the flying robot.
Its tentacle snaked around the machine
and squeezed tight. The drone was
crushed like an egg.

'Get out!' Amity yelled, racing for the
exit.

'What about Grunt?' Zelia asked.

The captain yanked open the door.
'There's nothing we can do. Move.'

She bundled the children out of
the shop and dived for cover as an
enormous tentacle smashed its way
through the window.

The kraken squeezed itself out into
the street, now six times its original
size. Its tentacles filled the narrow
passageway, clawing at the walls. It
opened its maw and roared, smashing
every window in the row.

They turned to run, but a tentacle
struck out, grabbing Mekki. The
Martian was lifted from the ground, his
arms pinned to his sides so he couldn't
grab his shock-prod.

Zelia turned, shouting his name, but was knocked from her feet by another feeler. She looked up to see Amity also in the kraken's clutches, her face darkening as a tentacle tightened around her.

Zelia grabbed a flash grenade and was about to launch the canister into the kraken's mouth when the gloom of the alleyway was lit by dozens of las-blasts.

The kraken screeched, dropping both Mekki and Amity to the ground. The captain leapt forwards, throwing herself across Zelia to shield her from the explosions. Mekki crawled towards them, keeping his head down low, as cannon fire lanced into the kraken, tearing the monster apart.

The barrage stopped as quickly as it had started. The air stank of charred meat, severed tentacles twitching where they had fallen. Zelia went to grab for the flash grenade that had tumbled from her hand, but Amity hissed at her to stay down until they were sure the bombardment was over.

When no more bolts were fired, the captain helped both children to their feet, and they turned to see three armoured warriors standing where the monster had been moments before. The same burst-cannons that had destroyed the kraken were now aimed at the crew of the *Profiteer*, muzzles glowing with deadly energy.

'Don't shoot,' Zelia said, raising her hands. 'We surrender.'

The largest of the warriors stomped

forwards, liquidised kraken squelching beneath armoured feet.

It stopped in front of Zelia, regarding her with a cluster of mechanical lenses.

'So, what happens now?' Amity asked. The warrior's angular helm snapped around to look at the rogue trader, its burst-cannon still raised.

'Now, you come with us,' it thundered.

'Do we have a choice?' Zelia asked.

The lens jerked back to face her. 'No.'

They were marched through the alleyways, the warriors clanking behind.

Zelia's arms ached, but she wasn't about to lower them if it meant being mown down in another burst of las-fire.

Faces appeared in shop windows as they passed, only to disappear as the onlookers spotted the warriors' weapons.

Zelia understood why. She'd recognised the battlesuits as soon as the dust had settled, from the strange hoofed boots to the missile launchers mounted on their broad, angular shoulders. The aliens were exactly how they had been described in Amity's records back on the *Profiteer*.

Zelia and the others had escaped being eaten alive by a hungry kraken, only to be captured by a squad of highly trained Tau warriors.

She didn't know whether to laugh or cry.

CHAPTER FOURTEEN

Lightbringer

The Tau herded their prisoners into an
elevator and ascended to what Zelia
assumed was one of the outpost's many
turrets. The doors opened and they
found themselves in rooms as airy and
light as the alleyways were narrow
and gloomy. Large panoramic viewports
dominated the walls, the stars sparkling
in the inky blackness of space. There
was technology everywhere, rows of
battlesuits standing to attention with
their backs to the windows. Their boxy
heads were lowered, mechanical eyes
dark. Zelia couldn't tell if they were
occupied or not.

A set of arched doors lay ahead, guarded by drones that swept aside as the prisoners were marched forwards. The doors opened automatically, revealing an even larger chamber filled with extravagant works of art. Glass sculptures hung beneath the high-domed ceiling, suspended by hidden hover-pads, while holo-paintings shimmered on the wall. Zelia didn't recognise any of the landscapes portrayed in the pictures, but there was no mistaking the blue-skinned female who reclined on a floating

lounger, her hulking bodyguard standing behind her. The wine in her goblet shimmered, changing colour from emerald green to rich purple, while serving drones hovered nearby, platters piled with food that seemed so self-consciously bizarre that Zelia suspected it existed to be marvelled at rather than consumed. The fruit shone, as if lit from within, while the selection of cold meats was sculpted to resemble extravagant erijabirds of every colour imaginable.

Not everything in the chamber was luxurious, though. Zelia glanced up to see a cage suspended from the high ceiling, a familiar shaggy shape behind the bars.

'Fleapit!' Zelia called out and the Jokaero let out a mournful wail.

'Silence!' the Tau shouted, and Fleapit slumped out of sight.

'What have you done to him?' Zelia demanded, but Amity reached out to stop her from charging straight for the Tau.

'Now, now,' the captain hissed. 'There's no need to yell at our host.'

Zelia looked at her in disbelief. 'Our *what*?'

Amity bowed low, doffing her hat. 'I apologise for my young friend. Her mouth runs away with itself. We're hoping she'll grow out of it soon.'

Zelia stared at the captain in shock.

'Ah, look. She's finally speechless. Wonders will never cease.'

Zelia's cheeks burned as the Tau chuckled.

'She's adorable,' the blue-skinned woman said, her lilting accent overemphasising each and every vowel. 'Is she yours?'

'No she is not!' Zelia snapped, appalled at the very idea.

'Unfortunately not,' Amity replied, the sarcasm in her voice clear for all to hear. 'My name is Captain Harleen Amity–'

'Of the *Profiteer*,' the Tau interrupted. 'My fame proceeds me.'

The Tau took a sip of her drink. 'I make it my business to know everyone who arrives on my station.'

'*Your* station?' Zelia asked. 'You own Hinterland?'

The Tau twirled the wine around her glass. 'In a manner of speaking. It is my home.'

'And who exactly are you?'

'Zelia...' Amity warned. 'Be nice.'

The Tau raised a hand. 'Don't trouble yourself, captain. We were all young and impertinent once.' She fixed her gaze on Zelia. 'I am Por-Vre Tolku Paxis.'

'That's quite a mouthful.'

The Tau inclined her head. 'Humans often find our names... challenging. You may call me Madame Lightbringer.'

Zelia could think of a few names she'd rather use, none of them polite.

'I like it,' Amity said before Zelia could find a new way to insult their host. 'After all, isn't that the Tau way? To bring light to all... for the Greater Good.'

Madame Lightbringer placed her glass on a floating tray. 'You know our teachings.'

Amity nodded. 'I've had dealings with the Tau from time to time... although I've never been marched through the streets by a squad of Tau warriors.' She glanced back at the battlesuits standing immobile behind them. 'That's a new one.'

Madame Lightbringer didn't seem fazed by the change in the captain's tone.

'You threatened one of my lady's clients,' rumbled her bodyguard.

Amity feigned innocence. 'I don't think so.'

Lightbringer pressed a control on the arm of her lounger. The captain's voice boomed over hidden vox-casters:

'*Selling alien livestock without a licence, and having a Tau drone at your beck and call? I may not have many friends these days, but I know a few inquisitors who would find your little operation particularly fascinating.'*

'You were spying on us?' Zelia said when the recording finished playing.

Madame Lightbringer steepled her fingers. 'My drones report everything they hear, even after they've been sold.'

'Sold?' Amity said, seizing on the word. 'So that's it. You're selling Tau technology to humans.'

'The exo-suits in the hangar bay,' Mekki realised. 'They are Tau.'

'Of the finest quality,' the bodyguard confirmed.

Amity shook her head in amazement. 'The secrets of the Tau Empire sold to the highest bidder. The Greater Good for the right price. I'm assuming it has been... simplified so us mere *gue'la* can hope to understand it.'

Madame Lightbringer raised a non-existent eyebrow. 'You speak our language?'

'A little. But may I say, your grasp of Low Gothic is impressive. I assume you've lived here a long time.'

'Ha. As if it would take long to master your tongue. Two or three *kai'rota* at most.'

'Two or three months?' Amity snorted. 'Most of the rabble on this station still struggle with it after a lifetime's practice.'

'Gue'la are naturally primitive,' she agreed. 'Which means, yes, we have to simplify our... wares.' She clicked her fingers and holograms appeared around her, a flickering catalogue of everything she had to offer, from powersuits to speeders.

'Perhaps you are interested in something, captain? Maybe some fresh *flo'tak* for that charming ship of yours?'

Amity laughed. 'I'm a little low on funds right now, but I'm certainly tempted.'

'I'm glad you approve.'

'And your people allow you to sell their technology to outsiders?' Zelia asked.

Madame Lightbringer threw back her

head and laughed as if that was the funniest thing she'd ever heard. 'Of course not. And who is going to tell them?' Lightbringer asked. 'You or your contacts in the Ordo Xenos?'

Amity had the decency to look shamefaced. 'Ah, yes. About that...'

'You were... how do you say... bluffing?'

Amity shrugged. 'You can't blame a girl for trying. My name *is* known to certain inquisitors, but not for the right reasons.'

Zelia couldn't believe what she was hearing. Amity had been lying all along? Well, two could play at that game.

'We could talk to the Tau instead,' she said quickly, 'tell them what you've been doing.'

Lightbringer laughed harder than ever. 'Oh, I like this one, captain. She has *shas* in her belly.' The Tau leaned forwards, fixing Zelia with a stare. 'And tell me, child, what exactly would you do? Open a direct vox to my home world? Contact the ethereals themselves?' Lightbringer examined Zelia carefully as she squirmed under the scrutiny. 'You don't even know who that is, do you?'

'We know what you are doing is wrong,' Mekki said, surprising everyone with his sudden interruption. The Martian pointed up at the cage near the ceiling. 'That is our friend. Karter had no right to sell him. Either you return him to us immediately, or I will broadcast this entire conversation to the Tau Empire. We will see what they have to say about you selling their technology to humans.'

Lightbringer just clapped her hands together in delight. 'Oh, very good. Very good. So passionate. So naive.' Her tone hardened. 'Unfortunately for you, I'm not as gullible as Milon Karter.' She glanced past her prisoners to address the battlesuits. 'Hold them.'

Metal hands grabbed their arms. Zelia

struggled, but it was hopeless. The battlesuits had a grip of iron. There was no way they could break free.

'Throw them out of an airlock,' Madame Lightbringer said, reaching across to select a translucent peach from her nearest serving-drone, its stone visible through its glassy flesh. 'Let's see them contact the Empire when the blood freezes in their veins.'

Zelia was lifted off her feet as the battlesuits turned to tramp back out of Lightbringer's chamber. She twisted and yelled, but it was no good. The suits marched forwards, metal fingers digging into their prisoners' arms, but stopped at the sound of a disturbance on the other side of the double doors. There was a clatter, followed by las-fire, and then the doors nearly flew off their hinges as they burst open.

Grunt charged in, swinging a severed kraken tentacle around his head like a slingshot.

'Down!' Amity yelled, as the heavy

feeler smashed into the battlesuits, removing all three of the warriors' helms from their heads in one swoop. Zelia craned around to see the faces of the Tau she had spotted in the marketplace. They barely seemed to register that they had been struck, still holding their prisoners' arms with their vice-like grips.

Not that they had to respond. Panels opened in the domed ceilings revealing armed drones that swept down from above, las-cannons firing. Grunt lashed out at them, knocking the first out of the air with the tentacle.

'Where did he come from?' Zelia asked, as Grunt took out another drone.

'There's a homing beacon in my belt buckle,' Amity said. 'Never leave the ship without it. Grunt, over here!'

The servitor whirled around, knocking Amity's captor off its feet. Amity rolled free, drawing her beamer and firing at point-blank range into the battlesuit's chest-plate.

Madame Lightbringer was on her feet, albeit standing behind her bodyguard, who had stepped protectively in front of her, sword drawn and ready to slice and dice anyone who came near.

'What are you waiting for?' she yelled. 'Destroy them!'

Through the open doors, the largest suit in the arsenal came to life and hefted its burst-cannon. Pivoting at its waist, it fired, a bolt of blistering energy slamming into Madame Lightbringer's bodyguard. The enormous

Tau was knocked back to crash into the back wall. He slid unconscious to the floor, smoke rising from his charred armour.

'What was *that*?' Lightbringer yelled, snatching up the bodyguard's dropped sword as the rogue armour lumbered through the open doors. 'Shoot at them, not me!'

Zelia cried out as the towering battlesuit raised its weapon to face her. She tried to wriggle free, but the battlesuit didn't open fire. Instead it stomped forwards, picking up speed. It was running straight for the Tau.

'Protect me,' Lightbringer shrieked.

Zelia's captor did as he was told, throwing her aside so he could prime his weapons. He never had a chance to fire. The marauding battlesuit twisted, slamming its shoulder into the smaller warrior's chest. The armoured guard was knocked to the floor, but before he could get up, the rogue Tau grabbed his leg to swing the fallen warrior like a club into the Tau that held Mekki. There was a sickening crunch as their heads cracked together, the stunned warriors slumping into a heap.

Mekki rolled free as one of the Tau tried to push himself up. Mekki snatched the shock-prod from his pack and thrust the prongs deep into the exposed circuitry at the Tau's neck. The battlesuit convulsed, voltage dancing over its servos, before it exploded, Mekki only just leaping clear.

'Woah!' a familiar voice thundered from the rogue battlesuit's vox. 'Way to go, Cog-Boy!'

Zelia's eyes widened as she recognised who it was.

'Talen? Is that you?'

The battlesuit responded by nearly stamping on Mekki.

'Whoops. Sorry about that.'

The metal giant was waving its arms wildly, plasma bolts streaming from its pulse-cannons. Some found their targets, reducing drones to flaming scrap, while

167

others shattered Madame Lightbringer's glass sculptures. The Tau threw herself to the ground as shards of glass peppered the walls.

'Help!' Talen's voice boomed from the armour. 'I can't control it! Somebody do something!'

CHAPTER FIFTEEN

Battle Stations

Everyone dived to the floor as Talen's armour turned on the spot, firing blindly. Debris and shrapnel was flying everywhere, bolts of energy destroying everything in their path. The third guard abandoned its tussle with Amity and rushed forwards, reaching for the burst-cannon just as the last remaining drone opened fire on Talen. The ganger turned, one of his flailing arms accidentally batting the Tau warrior into the drone's line of fire. The bolts strafed up the Tau's back and she tumbled forward, landing on her face. The drone prepared to fire until it was destroyed by a well-aimed shot from Amity's beamer.

'Zelia!' Talen thundered through the battlesuit's vox. 'Help me!'

Zelia looked across to Amity. 'Captain. Give me your beamer!'

The rogue trader scoffed. 'In your dreams.'

'Just do it!'

Amity threw her pistol over, and Zelia caught the weapon, turning to aim straight at Fleapit's cage. If anyone could help Talen, it was their furry friend.

She fired, but the bolt went wide, smashing into the ceiling instead.

'Again,' Amity shouted above the clamour of Talen's armour. 'You can do it!'

Her hands trembling, Zelia lined up her shot and pulled the trigger. This time the bolt sliced through the chain, and the cage tumbled to the ground. It bounced once, the door springing open. Fleapit leapt from his enclosure, landing on the battlesuit's shoulders. As the armour wheeled around, Fleapit went to work, yanking handfuls of cables from its innards.

'Stop!' boomed dozens of mechanical voices from the reception hall. Zelia looked around to see the rest of Lightbringer's battlesuits advancing on Talen, burst-cannons raised.

More by luck than judgement, Talen managed to turn and fire, hitting the first battlesuit to come through the door. It burst apart, but there was

no one inside! The armour collapsed like a puppet whose strings had been atomised.

'They're automated,' Zelia realised.

'That doesn't make them any less dangerous,' Amity cried, scrambling over to the doorway. She took one door, Zelia taking the other, and they pushed with all their might. The doors were heavier than they looked, but eventually slammed shut, blocking the attack. Amity bolted the lock, and called for Grunt to hold it tight. The servitor lumbered over, bracing himself against the doors.

Behind them, the chest of Talen's stolen battlesuit whirred open and the ganger clambered out, dripping with sweat.

'Remind me never to do that again,' he said as he flopped to the ground.

Zelia ran up to him and threw her arms around him. 'I thought we'd never see you again.'

Talen looked embarrassed before

returning the hug. 'As if you'd get rid of me that easily.'

'If you could leave the reunions for a less perilous moment,' Amity said, as metal fists pounded on the doors. 'Where's Lightbringer?'

The Tau was nowhere to be seen. 'She must have escaped when we weren't looking,' Zelia said.

'Which means there's another way out,' Amity said, prowling around the walls. 'We need to find it before those suits break down the doors.'

'And if we can't?' Talen asked.

Amity glanced at Fleapit, who was still elbow-deep in cables. 'Then you better pray the ape can get your suit working again.'

'He's not an ape,' Talen snapped. 'And even if he can, I'm not getting back in that thing. No way.'

'Why were you even in it?' Zelia asked.

'I followed Karter when he brought Fleapit to Madame What's-her-name,' he told her. 'I was waiting for the right moment to attack when you lot blundered in and ruined everything.'

'We didn't exactly have much choice in the matter,' Amity said, putting her back to the door to help Grunt.

'And none of this would have happened if you hadn't sold Fleapit in the first place,' Zelia pointed out.

'It was his idea!' Talen exclaimed.

'What?'

From the top of the battlesuit, Fleapit whooped and chattered in agreement.

'You were in this together?'

'We had a plan. I was going to rescue Fleapit as soon as Karter had told us about the Emperor's Seat. We didn't expect him to sell Fleapit straight away.'

'Why didn't you tell us?'

'Would you have believed me?' Talen said. 'Would you have even listened?'

The doors shook as the battlesuits continued to pound their way in.

'These things won't last much longer,'

Amity yelled. 'I hope you're ready for a fight.'

'Yes,' came a voice from behind Zelia. 'I am.'

Everyone turned to see Mekki standing in the stolen battlesuit.

'Mekki?' Zelia asked, staring at the Martian in disbelief. 'What are you doing?'

The chest-plate closed around Mekki's body so only his head showed. He looked vaguely ridiculous, framed by the armour's expansive shoulders.

'There is no way a human could pilot a Tau battlesuit correctly,' Mekki said.

Talen put his hands on his hips. 'I'd like to see you do better.'

'Then it is your lucky day, Talen Stormweaver.' Mekki glanced up at Fleapit, who was still perched on the armour's shoulders while the servo-sprite checked the suit's seals. Mekki nodded and Fleapit lowered the Tau helmet over the Martian's pale head. The helm clicked into place and its three red lenses flared into life. The battlesuit's hydraulics hissed and Mekki raised its arms, burst-cannons ready to fire.

'Ready?' Amity called up to him.

'Ready,' came the amplified reply.

Amity and Grunt ran from the doors as they blasted open, the bolt snapping in its lock. Lightbringer's automated army marched forwards, but Mekki opened fire, sending a volley of crimson bolts slamming into the attackers.

The battlesuits responded, but Mekki's

weapons were stronger. One by one, the battlesuits fell beneath Mekki's superior firepower. Zelia gripped the handle of Amity's blaster. This was going to work. They were going to get away.

'Cease firing, now!'

Madame Lightbringer's commanding voice cut through the battle. Zelia turned to see the Tau with the bodyguard's blade at Fleapit's throat. She hadn't escaped after all, but had been hiding until the moment was right.

'Mekki, do what she says,' Zelia called out, never taking her eyes from the Tau.

The battlesuit's cannons fell silent.

'A wise choice,' Lightbringer sneered. 'I would hate to destroy my own property, especially after I paid so much for him.'

Fleapit bared his teeth, but didn't respond. There was no telling if Lightbringer would make good on her threat.

'You fought well,' the Tau told them,

'but you lost, and now you all will die.'

'For the Greater Good?' Zelia asked.

'For *my* good,' Lightbringer replied. 'Take aim!'

The Tau's remaining battlesuits turned their weapons on the humans.

'You might want to save your energy,' Amity called out, holding up her hands. 'There's an even bigger battle on the horizon, one you'll never win.'

Lightbringer frowned. The captain hadn't raised her hands in surrender. She was making sure that everyone could see the ring on her index finger. The ring that was *flashing*.

'What is that?' the Tau hissed.

The captain glanced down. 'Oh, this? It's nothing much. Just a present from a friend.' A sly smile crept over her face. 'A friend in the Tau High Command.'

Lightbringer's nose-slit flared. 'What are you saying?'

'I'm saying that while Zelia might not know who to contact in the Tau

Empire, I have friends in very high places. The ethereals of Dal'yth knew that someone was selling Tau secrets to their enemies, and so hired a free agent to track down the traitor.' She waved her fingers.

'A free agent with a hidden vox,' Zelia said, looking at the flashing ring.

'And nothing to lose,' Amity confirmed. She glanced at her hand. 'By the look of things, the ethereals have got the message.'

The outpost shuddered, the rumble of multiple explosions reverberating through the station.

'People of Hinterland,' an alien voice boomed over every vox-caster at once. *'Your trading post has been claimed by the Tau Empire for the Greater Good of all. Put down your weapons and surrender.'*

The announcement was followed by the sound of distant cannons. The trading post's inhabitants were fighting back. The station rocked, the deck lurching beneath their feet. Zelia could hear las-fire on the deck below, saw flashes of light through the reception hall's viewports.

Madame Lightbringer didn't hang around to be captured. Dropping the blade, she ran for the elevator, her gowns billowing as she leapt over fallen battlesuits and downed drones.

'Zelia,' Amity shouted. 'My beamer.'

Zelia threw the las-pistol at the captain, who caught it and turned, aiming at the Tau merchant's back. She pulled the trigger, but the gun didn't fire.

'The power pack's exhausted!' She turned to Mekki. 'Your turn, Tech-Head.'

'No,' Talen said, his stolen bolas already spinning above his head. 'Leave this one to me.' He released the straps and the stones whirled towards Lightbringer. The Tau cried out as the leather thongs wrapped around her legs and she tumbled to the ground.

Lightbringer rolled onto her back and

tried desperately to untangle the straps.

'Going somewhere?'

She looked up to see the crew of the *Profiteer* standing over her. The armour-clad Mekki loomed over them all, his arm-cannon pulsing with energy.

'What are you going to do to me?' the Tau asked.

Zelia smiled. 'I think Fleapit has an idea about that.'

There was a grinding noise from behind, and Lightbringer looked down to see the Jokaero dragging his dented cage towards her, its door open... for now.

CHAPTER SIXTEEN

A Terrible Choice

The battle of Hinterland Outpost didn't last long. At first the station-dwellers fought back, but their spirit was soon broken as the initial wave of Tau starships was joined by a dozen more reinforcements. The Tau fleet surrounded the outpost, ion cannons primed and ready to fire, and Station Master Vetone reluctantly signalled the surrender.

Soon a Tau banner was flying from the space station's buttresses, its colours frozen in the cold vacuum of space.

Tau fire warriors marched through

the marketplace, clad in gleaming white armour. Every vox in the place was broadcasting a message from the Tau commander, declaring the station was now under the protection of the Tau Empire. The words were meant to sound comforting, with talk of freedom and liberation, but few on the station believed them, especially as the fire warriors rounded up any would-be freedom fighters and clamped them firmly in localised gravity bubbles.

Zelia looked at the prisoners uneasily as the elevator doors opened and Mekki stomped out, dragging a caged Madame Lightbringer behind him.

The marketplace was silent, most of the stalls abandoned. Cargo pods had been impounded by the Tau, and Zelia watched in horror as, accompanied by a message of peace and liberty, a spacefarer was stunned for wanting to protect his stack of very familiar barrels.

They were the same containers that

had housed Karter's kraken.

Whatever the contents of the stasis-barrels, the Tau had no right to seize other people's property. Regardless of what Zelia thought of the station, Amity had condemned the trading post to occupation. Zelia had doubts about the Imperium, but the Tau didn't seem any better. For all their talk about the Greater Good, the armoured warriors had conquered by force, winning the day because they had bigger, better weapons. They were the same as everyone else.

Not that Talen seemed to care. The ganger was scampering behind Amity like an excited puppy.

'So, you were recording the entire conversation?'

The captain nodded. 'Every word was transmitted back to Tau. I'd tipped them off as soon as we arrived, but the Dal'yth High Command wanted hard evidence that Lightbringer was here before seizing territory this near to the

Imperium.' She spotted an imposing Tau warrior in green armour and raised a hand in greeting. 'General Firebrand. It's good to see you again.'

The Tau bowed in acknowledgement. 'And you, captain. You have fulfilled your contract to the letter.'

Amity smiled. 'A pleasure doing business with you. Speaking of which, I believe this belongs to you.'

She nodded at Mekki, who dropped the cage at the general's feet. Madame Lightbringer glared up at the Tau officer.

Firebrand's lips curled up into a snarl. 'Por-Vre Tolku Paxis – you have dishonoured our people. The weapons of the Tau are forged for battle, not profit. You will be taken back to Dal'yth for trial.'

'What will happen to her?' Zelia asked.

'That is not my concern,' Firebrand replied. 'The ethereals will decide her fate.' He looked up at Mekki, ruby eyes narrowing. 'And this is one of the automated suits?'

'No,' Amity replied, rapping a knuckle on the golden chest-plate. 'A member of my crew is inside, but we will gladly hand it over, once payment is received, of course.'

'You will get what you deserve,' Firebrand said, aiming his pulse-cannon at Amity's head. The captain raised her hands.

'General, we had a deal.'

'I'm sorry,' the Tau told her, 'but no one outside the Empire must know of this dishonour. I am offering you and your crew a choice, captain. Either you stay here, as loyal citizens of our empire...'

'Sounds a lot like prisoners to me,' Talen snarled.

'Or identify yourself as an enemy of the Greater Good,' Firebrand continued, undaunted by the ganger's interruption.

'What happens then?' Zelia asked. 'A lifetime imprisoned in one of those gravity bubbles?'

'Or worse,' Mekki rumbled from within his battlesuit.

Amity seemed to consider it. 'It's a tempting offer...'

'But not one we can accept,' Talen told the general. 'We've got places to go...'

'And people to see,' Zelia said, grabbing the last flash grenade from her bandolier. She twisted the device, and threw it at the general's hoofed feet. 'Everyone, close your eyes!'

The grenade detonated, flooding the hangar bay with light.

'Run!' Amity yelled, and they charged for the hangar, Mekki making sure he shoulder-barged General Firebrand as he clomped by.

Pulse-cannons fired, but the blinded Tau warriors struggled to find their target. That wouldn't last. They needed another distraction, and Zelia knew exactly what to do...

'Mekki,' she called over her shoulder. 'See the barrels by the hangar bay doors?'

The armoured Martian guessed what she wanted him to do. He aimed his burst-cannon and fired, the bolt knocking the barrels into the air. When they crashed back down to the ground, the seals had buckled and dozens of claw-tipped tentacles burst out.

'That should keep them busy,' Zelia cheered, sliding underneath a rubbery limb. She looked up to see tentacles wrapped around dark green armour. The krakens were already growing, pulse-cannons raking their skin as the Tau fought back.

'What are you waiting for?' she yelled at the Hinterland inhabitants. 'This is your chance to take back your station!'

She smiled as a tentacle inadvertently swept through a gravity net, freeing prisoners who immediately took up arms and joined the fight.

'You're a proper little rabble-rouser, aren't you?' Amity said, as she lowered the *Profiteer*'s ramp.

Zelia and the others raced up the

gangplank, Mekki's armoured feet clanking on the metal. She grinned at Amity as they charged through to the flight deck. 'It's for the Greater Good.'

Amity swung into the pilot's chair. 'You won't be saying that when we get blasted to void dust by a Tau starship.'

Zelia looked through the viewport at the sleek cruiser that was laying siege to the space station. Any other day, Zelia would have said it was beautiful, a glistening manta ray ready to slice gracefully through the stars. For now, all she could see were the weapons that bristled along its shining hull, weapons that would strike the moment anyone tried to escape the Tau's 'protection'.

'Maybe we can outrun it,' Talen suggested.

'Of course we can outrun it,' Amity said, trying to pull the Tau ring from her finger. 'The *Profiteer* can outrun anyone, but thanks to this little trinket they'll be able to track us halfway across the Imperium. We need to destroy it.'

'No, wait,' Mekki said, unlocking the battlesuit and leaping down to the deck. 'Give it to me.'

Amity hesitated, but Zelia jumped in to support her friend.

'Just do it, captain. I don't know what Mekki's planning, but trust me, he's a miracle worker.'

'He better be,' Talen added, staring at the alien fleet.

Amity dropped the Tau ring into Mekki's hand. 'If we get atomised...'

'You will know who to blame,' Mekki said, dropping into the co-pilot's seat. Using the haptic implants on the tips of his fingers, he accessed the *Profiteer*'s vox-system. 'I need a sonic probe,' he told Zelia, flipping a magnifying lens down over his eyes. Zelia reached into his pack, found the right tool and passed it to Mekki, who used it to open an access port in the terminal.

'I hope you know what you're doing,'

the captain said as the Martian continued to vandalise her beloved dashboard.

'The ring is a transmitter, is it not?' Mekki asked, wrapping wires around the flashing band. 'I am preparing to transmit.'

'Transmit what?'

Mekki tapped his wrist-screen. 'Everything in my databank. Every catalogue, every recording, all delivered at exactly the same time.'

Dropping the ring into the access port, Mekki twisted the vox-control.

A shrill babble erupted from the speakers, dozens of voices speaking at once. With another twist, Mekki increased the volume so much that Zelia was sure the viewport would crack.

The words were distorted, playing over each other, but she could make out familiar voices in the mix. There was Mekki, of course, plus Talen and Erasmus. Her mum was there as well, even Zelia herself, every conversation in Mekki's archive played back at once and amplified beyond belief.

On the Tau cruiser, the commander pulled off his helm and threw it across the bridge. The noise was unbearable. He called over to his communications officer, but the order was lost in the tumult. Staggering over to a vox-terminal, he tried to raise General Firebrand on the trading post. It was useless. The signal was blocking every frequency. He looked up at the giant holo-screen which minutes before had shown the space station they had conquered for the Greater Good. Now all it displayed were flickering images of broken pots and rusty hunks of metal. There were faces, too. A young human girl and a pale-skinned boy.

The Tau commander slammed an armoured fist into the vox-controls. This couldn't be happening.

'How long before they block the signal?' Amity shouted over the din.

Mekki checked his read-out. 'Approximately thirty-nine point four three seconds.'

'Then we'd better get moving,' Amity said, priming the engines. 'Everybody, hang on.'

The *Profiteer* streaked out of Hinterland Outpost, zipping past the stricken starship and out into the stars. On the cruiser, the commander let out a sigh of relief as the bridge fell silent.

His ears rang, but he didn't care. The noise had stopped, that was all that mattered.

'Sir, I have General Firebrand,' the communications officer reported.

'Put him on screen.'

The commander turned, his eyes going wide as the general appeared. Firebrand's face was blackened, dark blood crusted around his nose-slit. The percussive beat of las-fire echoed from the speakers, followed by the roar of a gigantic beast.

We are under attack, the general yelled into his vox. *'Open fire on the station. I repeat, open–'*

The commander stared in disbelief as a huge tentacle wrapped around the general and yanked him away. The transmission cut out, the general's screaming face replaced with static.

The commander raced for his command chair. 'Y-you heard the general,' he barked. 'Arm gravitic launchers. Full power to primary railguns.'

The viewscreen shifted to a view of Hinterland Outpost. The station had deployed its cannons, which glowed bright in each gun turret.

'Well?' the commander snapped at his tactical officer. 'Where are my weapons?'

The Tau gunner blanched, his face going pale as he randomly pressed controls. 'They're not responding, sir. Internal communications were burned out by the transmission. Circuits have overloaded.'

The commander gripped the arms of his chair. 'Reroute power to forward batteries.'

'Sir, we can't. The central processor is offline. Controls are not responding.'

'Then make them respond! We will not fail. We are Tau. We are–'

His rant was cut off as Hinterland Outpost opened fire.

Harleen Amity's mouth dropped open as she listened to reports on a headset.

'What is it?' Zelia asked.

'If I heard correctly, Station Master Vetone just declared victory over the invading Tau forces.' The captain pressed buttons, attempting to boost the signal, but soon dropped the headset back down to the dashboard. 'We're out of range, but if that's true...'

'Mekki really is a miracle worker,' Talen grinned, slapping the Martian on the mechanical shoulder. 'Never doubted you for a minute, Cog-Boy.'

Amity consulted her controls to make sure they weren't being followed. 'Good work, everyone. You never know, carry on like this and you may even convince me that having a crew isn't so bad.'

Zelia slumped into an empty chair, suddenly exhausted. She watched as Amity took great pleasure in instructing Grunt to destroy the Tau communicator-ring. The servitor took the metal band in his cybernetic claw and crushed it between two pincers.

Meanwhile Mekki, Meshwing and

Fleapit descended on their stolen battlesuit, keen to learn its secrets.

Zelia couldn't believe how easily Mekki had adapted to wearing the armour. As she watched them work, she realised how little they really knew about each other. Mekki's past was a complete mystery to her. All those years travelling together, and she'd never even asked him why he left Mars. What had he meant by escape, and why did he have to fire a gun to do it? Then there was Fleapit. She knew he used to be a slave, but what had the Jokaero's life been like before he was captured? Where did he come from? How did he know how to make such incredible machines?

Even Talen, who was bombarding Amity with questions about her ship, was still a puzzle to Zelia. He could be so angry, so quick to think with his fists, and yet had risked his life to rescue Fleapit.

And then there was Captain Amity

herself, a woman who, by her own admission, 'had nothing to lose'.

A rogue trader, a ganger, a Martian, an alien and Zelia. Could they really be a crew?

'So,' Amity said, interrupting her thoughts, 'where now, my lady?'

'You're sticking with us, then?' Zelia asked.

The captain raised a pierced eyebrow. 'Until someone makes me a better offer.'

Zelia hoped she was joking. Either way, the rogue trader was right. They needed a destination.

'Talen?' she asked. 'What did Karter tell you?'

The ganger scratched the back of his head. 'To be honest, it didn't make much sense to me.'

'Does anything?' Mekki said, glancing up from the battlesuit.

'Oi!' Talen snapped, but the smile the boys shared was warmer than Zelia had ever seen. Maybe they were becoming a team, after all.

'Cut it out,' Zelia said, realising how much she sounded like her mum. 'Come on, Talen. Don't keep us in suspense. Where are we going?'

GALACTIC COMPENDIUM

PART THREE

XENOS

Pronounced 'zee-nos', this word is used throughout the Imperium to represent aliens. Known xenos races include the Necrons, Tyranids, Tau, Orks and Aeldari. Most are hostile, although there are a number of alien species that do not pose a direct threat to humanity.

That hasn't stopped the Imperium from condemning them. From an early age, Imperial citizens are taught to 'fear the alien', believing that all xenos races should be wiped out. There is even a shadowy organisation inside the Imperial

Inquisition known as the Ordo Xenos,
which has the authority to hunt and
destroy aliens wherever they are found.

CERAMITE

Ceramite is a heat-resistant material
used throughout the Imperium. It
can be found in starship hulls and
hive walls, although the highest grade
ceramite is reserved to construct
Space Marine power armour. In battle,
ceramite armour can protect its wearer
from energy-blasts and radiation.

SERVITORS

Millions of servitors
exist across human
space. Little more
than mindless drones,
the majority of these
lumbering slaves are
grown in genetic
vats and fitted with

cybernetic implants as soon as they are pulled from their tanks.

However, not all servitors are genetically engineered. Some were convicts and traitors who have had their minds wiped as punishment for their crimes. Converted against their will, they are forced to serve the Imperium with no memory of their past life.

ROGUE TRADERS

Smart-talking and trigger-happy, rogue traders live life on the edge, exploring the galaxy, trading, and even sometimes conquering alien worlds in the Emperor's name.

Most are loyal to the Imperium, but some are a law unto themselves. They pirate and pilfer, stealing what they want, when they want it. If caught, the punishment is severe. Stripped of their warrant of trade, they bring disgrace to their entire family. Abandoned by their crew, they become outlaws, surviving on their wits and whatever weapons they've stockpiled over the years!

THE TAU

Humans first encountered the Tau in the 35th millennium. Back then, the blue-skinned aliens were a primitive stone-age race who had only just mastered the creation of fire. Fast forward six thousand years, and they've evolved into one of the most technologically advanced races in the galaxy!

Unlike humans, the Tau have embraced artificial intelligence, creating all kinds of free-thinking drones. Travelling at night? A lume-drone will light your way. Need to send a message? Despatch a courier drone. Want a delicious meal? Order your chef drone to whip up a tasty treat. Facing an army of bloodthirsty Orks armed with more shootas than is strictly necessary? Then break out the mine drones, or the gun drones, or the shielded missile drones, or the... well, you get the idea.

Ruled by the mysterious ethereals, the Tau follow a philosophy called the Greater Good. They believe it is their duty to unite all species by conquering the galaxy. Join them and you can continue to follow your own way of life, as long as you submit to their rules.

DID YOU KNOW?

Humans who willingly join the Tau Empire are known as *gue'vesa* in the Tau language. The Imperium of Mankind brands anyone who submits to Tau rule as a traitor and heretic.

TAU WEAPONS

EMP grenades –
can send out an
electromagnetic
pulse that renders
technology useless.

Ion Cannons –
emit energy beams
that vaporise
enemies on impact.

Pulse Weapons –
fire highly
concentrated
plasma bolts.

Railguns –
projectile weapons
that fire solid
rounds.

CUSTODIAN-CLASS BATTLESHIP

Vehicle type: Tau Starship
Weapons: Railgun, Ion Cannons,
 Gravitic Launcher
Engine: ZFR Horizon Accelerator
 Engine
Can also carry smaller Warden-Class
 gunships into battle

TAU CASTES

Every Tau belongs to one of five
castes.
Shas: **The Fire Caste** – Strongest of
 all Tau, the Fire Caste are warriors
 and fighters.
Kor: **The Air Caste** – Unsurprisingly,
 the *Kor* provide pilots to Tau forces.
Flo: **The Earth Caste** – These
 are the engineers, technicians and
 farmers of the Tau Empire.
Por: **The Water Caste** – Diplomats
 and merchants. They are also
 masters of manipulation. Never try

to trick a *Por*. It rarely works!

Aun: The Ethereals – The ruling class of the Tau Empire. Disobey them at your peril!

Changing or leaving your caste is strictly forbidden. Some sources say that it's a crime that is punishable by death, but that may be human propaganda.

TAU ALPHABET

A	-	⊐	M	⊓
B	-	⊡	N	⊓
C	-	⊐	O	⊏
D	-	⊐	P	⊡
E	-	⊓	R	⊓
F	-	⊔	S	⊐
G	-	⊏	T	⊤
H	-	⊔	U	⊔
I/Y	-	⌐	V	⊔
J	-	⊒	X	♪
K	-	⊐		
L	-	⌐		

10 THINGS YOU NEED TO KNOW ABOUT THE INQUISITION

1. The Inquisition is a secretive organisation feared throughout the Imperium of Man.

2. Its members are called inquisitors, a secret police force that answer only to the Emperor himself.

3. The Inquisition's origins are shrouded in mystery. Not even the inquisitors themselves know how their organisation came into being, although many believe it was founded 10,000 years ago by Malcador, the First Lord of Terra and one of the Emperor's closest advisors.

4. The Inquisition has no official leadership. Each inquisitor is free to interpret the law as he or she sees fit.

5. Each inquisitor is given an Inquisitorial Seal. It is a symbol of their absolute authority.

6. Inquisitors have the power to convict

any Imperial citizen. They can even order the destruction of an entire planet, known as 'Exterminatus'.

7. Disobeying an inquisitor is a crime punishable by death.

8. The Inquisition is split into three main orders, or ordos. The Ordo Hereticus (Witch Hunters), Ordo Malleus (Daemon Hunters) and Ordo Xenos (Alien Hunters).

9. An inquisitor will often take on an apprentice, or acolyte. If they serve their master well, acolytes may eventually become inquisitors in their own right.

10. Many inquisitors are psykers, beings born with psychic abilities such as telepathy or the power to move objects using only their mind. Some can even summon fire.

SERVO-SKULLS VS TAU DRONES

SERVO-SKULLS

- Robotic devices housed in a human skull.
- Some servo-skulls have the ability to speak, but they are not capable of individual thought.
- Often fitted with telescopic mandibles and pincers.
- Lingua-Vox servo-skulls are able to translate thousands of languages and are often used by explorers and diplomats.

TAU DRONES

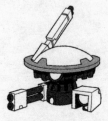

- Sleek disc-shaped machines.
- Tau drones possess artificial intelligence, and are able to think for themselves.
- Can be fitted with a wide variety of apparatus from weaponry to surgical equipment.
- Escort drones assist Tau diplomats in delicate negotiations with other races, including humans.

DID YOU KNOW?

In the Tau language, drones are called *kor'ves*, which means 'faithful helper'.

ABOUT THE AUTHOR

Cavan Scott has written for such popular franchises as *Star Wars, Doctor Who, Judge Dredd. LEGO DC Super Heroes, Penguins of Madagascar, Adventure Time* and many, many more. The writer of a number of novellas and short stories set within the *Warhammer 40,000* universe, including the *Warhammer Adventures: Warped Galaxies* series, Cavan became a UK number one bestseller with his 2016 World Book Day title, *Star Wars: Adventures in Wild Space – The Escape.* Find him online at www.cavanscott.com.

ABOUT THE ARTISTS

Cole Marchetti is an illustrator and concept artist from California. When he isn't sitting in front of the computer, he enjoys hiking and plein air painting. This is his first project working with Games Workshop.

Magnus Norén is a freelance illustrator and concept artist living in Sweden. His favourite subjects are fantasy and mythology, and when he isn't drawing or painting, he likes to read, watch movies and play computer games with his girlfriend.

STORIES FROM THE FAR FUTURE

WARPED GALAXIES

An Extract from book four
War of the Orks
by Cavan Scott
(out November 2019)

Hinterland Outpost was a wreck. Smouldering cruisers littered the landing bay, once-precious cargo scattered among the wounded and dying. Inquisitor Jeremias marched up to a medic who was doing her best to tend to a wounded docker. One glance told the inquisitor that the injured man wasn't long for this world. Jeremias had experienced many battlefields and knew a lost cause when he saw one.

'What happened here?' he asked,

and the medic jumped at the unexpected question. She turned, her eyes widening as she took in Jeremias's Inquisitorial rosette and the servo-skull floating at his epauletted shoulder.

'There was an attack,' she said, turning back to her patient. 'The Tau.'

Jeremias's mouth curled into a snarl. 'The Upstart Empire. Here. And you fought them off?'

The woman didn't answer.

'Well?'

She glared up at him. 'Look, I'll answer your questions, but only after I've treated this man. His wounds are serious.'

'His wounds were terminal,' Jeremias corrected her.

She looked back to the docker and sighed. The docker had gone.

Jeremias watched as she pulled out a cracked data-slate and recorded his time of death. The woman was impressive. Not many citizens would stand up to an inquisitor, even in such grave situations. She had spirit.

The medic closed the man's unseeing eyes and stood to address Jeremias. 'Yes,' she said, wiping blood from her hands on to a rag that looked decidedly unsanitary. 'We fought back, for all the good it did us. The power grid is on its last legs, and most of the station's occupants are dead or dying.'

'But you didn't fall to the xenos scum,' Jeremias pointed out. 'Praise the Throne.'

She repeated the oath, although her words were hollow. 'Is that why you're here?' she asked. 'Is the Imperium sending aid?'

He raised an immaculate eyebrow, and the woman scowled.

'I mean...' she stammered, her expression hardening, 'I realise that's not what you people do...'

'"You people"?'

'The Inquisition. I just thought...

seeing what happened here...'

Jeremias looked around the wrecked landing bay. 'Hinterland Outpost has long been a cesspool of villainy and heresy, operating outside the Emperor's law. It is good that you fought back against the Tau, but even if supplying aid was within my duties, I see little worth saving.'

Her mouth dropped open. 'How can you say that? People are dying here. *Humans* are dying here.'

His eyes paused on a nearby corpse. It was a Kroot, its alien tongue lolling from a beaked mouth. 'Was that one of the Tau's retinue?'

She glanced at the fallen alien. 'No. That was Skrann. He worked here, unloading cargo. He was a decent sort.'

Jeremias saw her flinch at her own words, and for good reason.

'Xenos working alongside humans,' Jeremias said, his tone judgemental. 'And you don't see a problem in that?'

'All I meant was—'

He raised a gloved hand to stop her. 'I know what you meant, but the argument is moot. There's an old Terran saying – "You dug your trench, you sleep in it." This is your problem, not the Imperium's.'

'So if you're not here to help...?' The medic left the question hanging. Her insolence was beginning to grate.

'I am looking for survivors of a recent tragedy in the Segmentum Pacificus. Three children. A girl and two boys.'

Her eyebrows shot up. 'Segmentum Pacificus? But that's—'

'A long way from here – yes, yes it is. I have reason to believe that they travelled here.'

The medic's eyes narrowed. 'To Hinterland. Why? *How?*'

'It is forbidden to question an inquisitor's methods,' snapped Corlak, Jeremias's loyal servo-skull.

He waved away his familiar's

outrage. 'Have you seen them?' he asked the woman.

The medic laughed bitterly. 'Have I seen children? On Hinterland? I'll tell you what I've seen. Bodies. Lots and lots of bodies. And that number increases with every hour. Our medical supplies were destroyed in the attack. I have nothing to work with. And you're asking me about *children*?'

This was getting him nowhere. He turned away, looking for someone else to question.

'No... wait. *Please.*'

A hand grabbed his arm and pulled him back. The woman had actually touched him! He swung around, pushing her back. She stumbled, falling onto the body of the man she had tried to save.

'That was your last warning,' he barked at her. 'I suggest you stay down.'

'I'm sorry...' the medic said, visibly shaking. 'I just... all this... it's too much. The Emperor...'

'The Emperor will protect you from darkness,' he interrupted. 'Now go about your work.'

She nodded and started picking up her supplies. Jeremias watched her for a moment. Was she right? Should he help? *Could he?* No. This was not his mission.

He turned, aware of Grimm – his cyber-mastiff – watching from the ramp of his ship. The hound looked ready to charge, to attack the woman for daring to touch him. The inquisitor raised a hand and the mechanical beast stalked back up the ramp, cybernetic eyes glowing red.

She had learned her lesson. She would do as he said, helping the survivors of the battle. She had her duties... and Jeremias had his.

The inquisitor looked around. The tech-savants had vanished, no doubt spooked by the altercation. Jeremias sighed. He would have to venture deeper into the station to find someone to question. The children had come here. Of that, the visions had been clear.

'Looking for the kiddies, are you?'

The voice was gruff, unrefined. Jeremias turned to see a goat-faced Beastman sitting beneath the wreck of a skimmer. The abhuman smiled, showing uneven brown teeth. 'I can tell you about the kids, if you can get me off this dump?'

Jeremias's eyes narrowed. 'I'm listening...'